DARK MOON

DREAMS OF REVENGE

Other Thrillers
you will enjoy:

Kiss of Death (Dark Moon #1)
by Elizabeth Moore

The Mummy
by Barbara Steiner

The Phantom
by Barbara Steiner

Silent Witness
by Carol Ellis

Twins
by Caroline B. Cooney

DARK MOON

DREAMS OF REVENGE

ELIZABETH MOORE

SCHOLASTIC INC.
New York Toronto London Auckland Sydney

ISBN 0-590-25510-X

Copyright © 1995 by Barbara Steiner.
All rights reserved. Published by Scholastic Inc.

12 11 10 9 8 7 6 5 4 3 2 1   5 6 7 8 9/9 0/0

Printed in the U.S.A.   01

First Scholastic printing, July 1995

Prologue

In a single, violent motion, Rebecca tore the black velvet choker she was wearing from her neck and threw it to the ground. Where the choker had been was a hideous, twisted scar.

For a moment Jeffrey was so shocked he was unable to make a sound. Then he gasped, "Rebecca." He wanted to turn his head away from the terrible sight, but he couldn't take his eyes off the ghastly scar.

"What happened to you, Rebecca? Who did this to you? Why?" Jeffrey asked in an anguished voice, taking hold of her arms.

Rebecca gazed steadily at Jeffrey, taking in the horrified expression on his face. "I, too, know what it is to be falsely accused," she said, her voice low and mysterious. "You think that you have known betrayal and despair, but it's *nothing* compared to what I have endured."

Rebecca's face twisted into a mask of rage.

"I've waited a long, long time for my revenge. Now my plan is finally coming true, and my soul will have some peace."

Rebecca pulled away from Jeffrey. She saw the deep sadness on his face, and her lips curved in a smile of wicked satisfaction.

"I know you love me, Jeffrey. Your love for me is so great that it's almost more than you can bear. And now I will make sure that love will torture and torment you."

Jeffrey watched Rebecca turn and walk away, floating through the mist. A horrible feeling of emptiness overcame him. Inside, he felt something break and die.

"Jeffrey," Rebecca called back to him through the swirling mists. "My nightmare is almost over. But yours is just beginning."

Chapter 1

I stand in the courtyard beside the gallows, the heavy noose around my neck. The rope burns and chafes my skin. My hands are tied so tightly together that there is no feeling left in either one. Would that I had no feeling in any of my body.

Why am I tied? Do they think I can escape from them now? Do they think I have the strength to run, to hide, even to deny their accusations?

A flame of anger burns deep inside me. I know I am innocent of the charges they have dreamed up. I know what they are doing to me and to others is more evil than any sin I have committed. They say that I am evil, yet evil lives in each and every heart of those who are watching, those who are accusing me.

A man, looking very important in his black suit, reads out a list of all my crimes.

I have caused Goody Bayley's cow to dry up,

to stop giving milk to her family and the calf it needs to nurse.

I have bewitched Goody Carter's goats so they broke out of their pen and lost themselves in the woods.

I caused Ernest Burton's expensive bull to become frenzied, break through his fence, and disappear without a trace.

I cannot stay still and listen one minute longer. I tip my head back and laugh and laugh and laugh. I hear myself. The laughter sounds like that of an insane person, filled with hysteria and denied fear rather than humor. I cannot stop. I will not allow myself to cry or beg and plead, so I laugh.

John Warden frowns at me. Other men nod and look at each other as if this proves the accusations are true. Their women cover their mouths and look at me with loathing and disapproval.

When I am able to stop laughing, I realize I have broken the rules for proper behavior at a serious moment. This is not the correct attitude for a woman accused of witchcraft. I should bow my head and ask for forgiveness. I should confess my sins.

What I wish I could do is convince others to see the horror of what is happening in Salem. I should ask them to come to their senses and *stop these crimes they are committing. But who would listen? They would write off my pleas as the ravings of an insane woman.*

My eyes focus on Caleb Thomas, come to watch the finish of what he started. I hate this man who sat in judgment at my trial, who made a mockery of anything I could say in my defense. Who listened to the prattlings of old women, envious of my beauty, young women jealous because all the men looked at me instead of them. They hated me because my skin was fair and without blemish, my lips a natural red, my hair long and dark and curling slightly in the eternal dampness of New England's climate.

Knowing I have but little time, I lift my head and straighten my shoulders.

I toss my head and flaunt my thick mass of curls, wishing I had been allowed to wash my hair and bathe my body before today.

The act of regaining my pride and my confident manner makes me defiant and angry all over again. I have nothing to lose.

I scream at them all, then continue my insane laughter.

Rebecca continued to laugh as she returned to the present and stared out over the cliffs at the roiling ocean. The memory had done its job. She knew why she had come back. She burned with the anger she needed to continue.

The fog swirled around her and cleared slightly. Coming toward her was Jeffrey Thomas, his face puzzled, his manner sufficiently apologetic. Tipping her head back she laughed again, delighted with the effect she had on this man.

Jeffrey Thomas had no understanding of why Rebecca had run away from him. And why she had talked of a nightmare beginning for him. Her agony finished, his just begun. What was she talking about? What had he done? How had he offended her? It was obvious that he had. He was not used to women being offended by a kiss, a kiss he thought she had welcomed, invited.

Deep inside, he wished he could run. Run to his car, jump in, drive with no concern for the speed limit, be concerned only with escaping. Deep inside he wanted to escape from this woman who acted like no woman he had ever known.

But he couldn't. He loved Rebecca Webster. Despite every reason he had to stay away from her, he couldn't leave her.

She was angry. Why couldn't he be angry, too? He didn't know.

The fog that swirled around him chilled him

to the bone, clogged his brain with cotton, and filled him with fear.

Rebecca had run and the cliffs were nearby. In this mist she could inadvertently fall. It had happened before.

"Rebecca, where are you?" he shouted. "Don't move. Stay where you are until I find you."

Watching his own footing, he started in the direction she had fled. He tested each step, making sure he was on solid ground. Twice rocks loosened and tumbled off the slope, dirt splattering and spilling behind them, as if the fog chewed off tiny bits of the cliff, spitting it out to cascade into the ocean.

"Don't move. I'll find you," he called again, feeling frantic.

Never had he seen fog this thick. He felt as if he were clawing his way through masses of wet spiderwebs that clung to his face and hid the world he knew.

Suddenly, up ahead, the fog swirled and parted, letting him see as if into the future.

Rebecca stood, gazing out over the ocean, a hypnotic look on her face. She appeared to be in a trance, not in this world. Around her the light was luminous, glowing, unearthly.

In one hand the black velvet ribbon from her neck, the ribbon that hid an awful secret, trailed, curling slightly in the breeze, weaving back and forth like a trapped serpent.

He stopped, frozen in place, not daring to walk closer, not daring to call out to her. One more step and she would be over the cliff. She would be dashed to her death on the rocks below.

He watched her until she started to laugh, tipping her head back. He shivered, unsettled by the sound that touched him deeply, not even knowing why it touched him as it did.

He wanted desperately to take her in his arms, comfort her, make her stop laughing. Make her love him.

At last she became silent. Lifting the ribbon, she tied it back in place around her neck. She turned then, saw him standing, watching her. She smiled and beckoned to him.

Nothing — not one thing in the whole world could have stopped his moving to take her in his arms.

Chapter 2

"Rebecca, are you all right? I was frantic, worrying." Jeffrey caught her up in an embrace that he wanted to continue forever.

Her chilled body warmed against his and neither spoke until she stopped shaking.

"What happened?" He whispered into the soft hair around her face. "Why did you say the things you said and run away from me?" The exotic smell of her perfume filled his nostrils and made him dizzy. His fingers gently touched the ribbon, and he remembered the awful scar underneath. "What happened to you, Rebecca?" He repeated the question with another meaning. "What caused this scar?"

"I'm not ready to tell you, Jeffrey. Just hold me, hold me for a little longer."

"I don't ever want to let you go." Jeffrey pulled her closer. She could keep all the secrets she wanted. Her past didn't matter to him. Why should he care when he loved her so much right now?

The wind whipped around them, pushing the fog out to sea, tugging at Rebecca's skirts, which flapped softly around them. Jeffrey's fear receded a little and he relaxed, knowing that whatever had made Rebecca angry, it was not him. It had to be a memory, a memory of something she didn't want to think about.

He resolved not to pry, not to mention the scar again. If she wanted to talk, surely she knew he was there to listen.

After a few minutes he dared whisper, to make sure, "You aren't angry with me, are you, Rebecca?"

"Now why would I be angry with you, Jeffrey?" She pulled away, stepped back a step and stared at him, smiling. Her violet eyes were warm again.

"I don't know, but you can talk to me, Rebecca. You can tell me anything. You know that, don't you? If you need to talk about something awful that happened to you in the past, I'll listen. And if you need to keep it secret, I'll do that, too. I'm always here for you, Rebecca."

"I know." She turned and walked away from him. He followed her, not exactly liking the tone of her voice. He wouldn't stay if she hated him, if she really was angry with him. He didn't think she was, but she was so hard to read.

He'd never had to wonder what Barbara was thinking, guess at how she was feeling. She was so easy to be around, so comfortable to be with.

Too comfortable? a little voice inside him asked. *Were you bored with Barbara? Was that why it was so easy to let her go and fall in love with Rebecca?*

He didn't want to think about Barbara. She was gone. He had loved her, but now she was gone. If she hadn't been killed on his boat, he would probably have broken up with her over Rebecca. But that happens, doesn't it? People break up. Even people who've gone together for a long time. He might have felt guilty for a short time, afraid he'd hurt Barbara. But she would have understood. She wouldn't have wanted him to stay around if he loved someone else.

Now, he had to put her out of his mind. The police were no longer questioning him about Barbara's death. Even when her body washed ashore with marks on her neck, there was no evidence that Jeffrey had strangled her.

Sometimes he wondered how he could love two such different girls. Maybe he hadn't really loved Barbara. Maybe what he thought was love was just a comfortable friendship. He'd started going with her when he was so young, he didn't know what love was.

Is love being obsessed by someone? Afraid half the time you're around them?

"You're awfully quiet all of a sudden, Jeffrey," Rebecca said, stopping to stare out over the ocean. "Penny for your thoughts." She moved close to him, causing him to catch his breath.

"Not worth it." He grinned and reached for her. She skipped away.

"Let me guess." She turned and walked backward, tossing her long, dark hair aside when the wind swept it across her face. "You were wondering how I happened to come along just when I did. And how I happened to fall in love with you. What you did to deserve it."

He reached for her. She twisted away again.

"You are so easy to read, Mr. Thomas. How could I not know what you feel?" Her dark eyes flirted with him.

"You have bewitched me." He laughed.

"Don't say that." Her mood shifted again. She turned. Her body stiffened, and she walked faster.

"What did I say?" He hated games when he didn't know any of the rules. He tried to continue teasing her. "If I live a million years, I will never understand women. At an early age they learn to cast spells over men, then when someone accuses them of doing it, they deny they'd *ever* do such a thing."

"You make me sound like someone — something evil. A person that can conjure up magic and use it for her own purposes."

The only way Jeffrey knew how to change the subject was to apologize, even though he'd done nothing wrong — that he knew of. "I'm sorry. You're not evil; you're not manipulative; you didn't *make* me fall in love with you. I did it all on my own, all by myself. You had absolutely nothing to do with it."

Rebecca had to smile at Jeffrey's words. She knew she had him so confused that he was afraid to say anything. She knew he was so much in love with her that he'd do anything for her. That was what she wanted. Wasn't it?

Hadn't she come back to get revenge? And what better revenge than to make Jeffrey love her desperately, then hurt him. She had to think of a way so he'd never forget her. So he'd never be the same — as she would never be the same.

The one thing she hadn't counted on was falling into her own trap. She hadn't counted on falling in love with Jeffrey. She would *not* fall in love with this man. She would not let him comfort her. He would *not* make her forget the past and forgive him. She wouldn't. She couldn't!

"No!" she shouted. "No, I will not fall in love with you. I won't!"

Suddenly, the fog came back to the shore and surrounded them with thick clouds that allowed Rebecca to escape and hide.

She dashed across the rocky ground and jumped into her car. Twisting the key to bring the engine to life, she shifted down and roared away. She had to get away for a time. She had to regain her courage, her resolve. She had to remember all her many reasons for returning to seek out and destroy Jeffrey Thomas.

Chapter 3

Rebecca drove like a madwoman until she was halfway to town. She and Jeffrey had been planning to go someplace and eat. She wasn't quite sure why she had picked this time, that place — the cliffs near her house — to reveal her scar.

What good had that done? Well, it had stopped the loss of control she had over her emotions. It had reminded her that falling in love with Jeffrey Thomas was not on her agenda. She had needed to be reminded of her mission, but showing Jeffrey her scar had not given her the satisfaction she had thought. It had just made Jeffrey treat her more gently. Made him worry about her and how she had gotten hurt.

But nothing was going to change the past.

She swung into an overgrown pull-out where a trail led to the ocean, and stopped the car. She took several deep breaths in order to calm down.

The cold, damp fog that swirled into the car and wrapped around her took her back to another place even colder, even damper.

I huddle in my bed, trying to keep warm. The wealthier prisoners have wood and a fire. They have food. I remember the taste of rich, warm soup. My mouth waters and my stomach rumbles at the thought. My last meal was bread made from weevily flour and water, dirty water. I crave a cup of tea. What I wouldn't give for a sweet, hot cup of tea. Not meaning to, I sob and groan.

Before I can hide my misery, Mercy Smith sits on my bed and pats my back until I stop crying. Her little daughter, Dorcas, sits and sings to her doll, which our jailers have let her keep.

I try to lift my spirits for Mercy and Dorcas. And, I am still alive. Patience Clark was taken from our cell today. We know she was on her way to the gallows. We know we will never see her again. Patience was in prison simply because she had red hair. She told us that her accusers claimed that flames came from her head. Her hair was lovely, not unlike a candle flame, glittering and sparkling in our occasional shaft of sunlight.

It has been raining for days. Water stands in our cell, in some places to our ankles. The smell of mold and decay fills our nostrils. We are never free of it. The dampness seeps into our clothing, our bedding, our very bones.

I pull my shawl tighter around my shoulders and sit up. There is nothing to occupy our time. We are talked out. I stare at the light from the one candle we have left. Mercy hopes her husband will be able to find a little money for more or we will sit here in the dark and wait.

That is the worst part — the waiting. Neither of us has had a trial, so we think we can't be hanged until we are tried and declared guilty.

A noise in the hallway alerts us that something is happening, someone is coming. A woman is led to our cell. She stands, sobbing, while the jailer opens the cell door. Behind her a man appears with wood and matches, a basket of food and candles. I stare at the woman's clothing and realize that she is not poor, that her family has sent these things with her.

I hate myself for thinking it, but I wonder if there is tea in the basket. What food does she have? She will share. We have all shared our meager belongings.

"You, come here." One of the men points to me.

"Me? Why? What do you want of me now?" I try to make my voice hard and without fear.

"There is no room here for four. You will come with us."

He doesn't give me any choice. I hesitate, but he takes my arm, twisting it until I cry out with pain.

"We don't mind being crowded." Mercy Smith tries to get them to leave me there.

The new woman looks up and stops crying. "I don't want Rebecca Webster here. Take her away, anyplace but here."

I stare. The new prisoner is Goody Lyman, the woman who first accused me of being a witch. Now someone has brought the same fate to her.

I try, but I take no joy in seeing her here, brought down to my level after she pointed her finger at me. I hate her, though, for making me leave the place I have gotten used to, the kindness of Mercy Smith.

Mercy stares at me, her huge eyes sad and gentle. She reaches out to touch my arm, but a man pushes her aside.

I walk along the dark hallway to another cell. When I see where they take me, I dig in my heels and try to protest. "No, no, I cannot, I cannot."

Both men laugh. "Perhaps we can hurry your trial. Would you like that? We could hurry you on your way to the hanging tree."

The door before me creaks open, then slams behind me. I find myself in a new cell that is only of a size that allows me to stand. The size of an upright coffin box. I have no bed, no fire, no candle, nothing. I cannot even lie down, but must stand or crouch on the floor. The only thing worse would be to be chained to the wall as is the slave Tituba.

The moment the door closes, leaving me only a foot-square window through which to peer into the dark hallway, I feel I cannot bear this. Four cold, damp stone walls press closer and closer in on me. Surely there is not enough air to keep me alive. I gasp and choke until I am calm enough to breathe steadily. I will endure this, I will. It is only my imagination that I cannot breathe.

The older of the guards returns first. "Here — I will do you this favor. But remember you will owe me a favor in return." He sets a stub of candle in the window between two iron bars and lights the wick. I may have an hour of light at the most. I pray I can use that hour to grow accustomed to this new torture.

The second, and younger, of the guards on duty also stops and peers in at me. He grins, showing his rotting teeth, blowing his stinking breath toward me.

"And I have someone to keep you company. You will thank me, too, at some later date." He cackles, then tosses something through the bars into my cell.

Two red eyes peer up at me from the floor. A sharp, pointy nose moves back and forth, sniffing. A rat! The man has tossed a live rat into my tiny cell!

Rebecca returned to the present still shaking. She remembered how she had kicked and stomped with her bare feet. She felt the pain from the bite the rat landed before it was dead. She pulled her foot under her and rubbed it to forget the torn flesh. She shuddered, wanting to huddle there in the car and cry.

Instead, she started the car's engine, put it in gear, and screeched backward into the road.

Hatred and the desire for revenge churned in her stomach, sent determination through her entire body. She would seek out Jeffrey Thomas and finish the job she had come to do.

Chapter 4

Jeffrey heard the car door slam, the engine of the sleek, red convertible roar to life. He ran toward the sound. He was too late. He heard the car barrel down the road, but he didn't even get a glimpse of it through the thick fog.

He had stumbled through the woods to the road, narrowly missing trees and tree limbs. The fog had an eerie light to it and was icy cold. The dampness seeped straight through his lightweight polo shirt.

He continued on the path to the old house where he had left his own car. Getting in, he turned the ignition key and heard only a click. He stomped on the accelerator, shooting some gas into the line. Then he tried again. A click, a growl, then nothing. Why wouldn't his car start? It was running fine when he came up here. He knew he had plenty of gas. He had filled the tank yesterday.

Had he flooded it? Once more he tried to get the car to start. Not even a click this time. He pounded on the steering wheel in frustration.

Rebecca couldn't have known his car was dead, but she had left him, stranding him here. How dare she? It was miles to town, and a storm was fast approaching.

He would not stay and wait for her to come back, then beg for a ride. He didn't want her to have that satisfaction. But he had no other choice but to walk, or jog. Jogging would keep him warm. Get him out of the woods before the storm hit. No one would be driving up here on a day like this. He could never hope for a ride.

If he could get to the intersection of the highway, there was a small general store and a phone. He could call — whom? He could call Miranda or Paul. One of them would come after him.

He started downhill. The day became darker and darker until late afternoon was as dim as dusk. Flashes of lightning hit all around him. He wasn't much of a runner, but he picked up his pace. The last thing he wanted was to be caught out here in a downpour. And the storm seemed unusually fierce. Even though Rebecca had made him angry by leaving him, he hoped she got back to town, or wherever she went, before the storm hit. Driving on this mountain road could be dangerous enough without adding a thunderstorm.

The first drops began just as he dashed into the small gas station and general store.

"Hey there, boy. You narrowly missed getting drowned." An old man perched on a high stool, staring out the window at the downpour. "This came up mighty fast, didn't it? Unexpected, too. Day was as pretty as a picture till 'bout an hour ago."

Jeffrey stared out the window and counted himself lucky. He would have been drenched in seconds.

"Car break down?" The old man wanted to talk.

"You could say that." Jeffrey rubbed down the goose bumps on his arms. "Can I use your phone?"

"Local call?"

"Just into town."

"I reckon I can afford that." The man grinned and headed to the back of the store, pointing to the phone behind the counter and the register.

Jeffrey had to stare at it for a minute before he could call. He hadn't seen an old black rotary phone in some time. He stuck his finger in the first hole and managed to dial Paul's number. No answer, not even a machine. Then he dialed Miranda, hoping for better luck.

She answered.

"Miranda, thank goodness." He was relieved to hear her voice. She'd give him a bad time over this, but if she'd come and get him, he'd pay that price. "Listen, don't ask me how or why, but I'm stranded out on the highway. Can you come get me?"

"The highway that you turn off of to go to where Rebecca is living?" She started right in on him. The tone of her voice said, Serves you right for chasing after her.

"Yes, that highway. Just come get me, will you? Please?"

"Well, I guess I can spare the time. I thought I'd paint my fingernails, but, if it's an emergency, I — "

"It's an emergency. Listen, though, maybe you'd better wait until this storm lets up some."

"What storm?"

"It's not raining in town?"

"Not a drop. Sunny day, beautiful. Not a cloud in the sky." Miranda's voice had a musical quality that made him start to feel better.

"That figures. Come right now, will you?"

"I'm on the way, Jeff. Sit tight."

What else could he do? He was pleasantly surprised to see the old man heading for him, a cup of steaming coffee in hand.

"On the house, considering the weather." The man handed Jeffrey the mug, the coffee creamed to a toffee color, just the way he liked it.

"My friend says it's not raining in town." He sipped the hot liquid and felt better at once.

"That's strange, ain't it?" The old man moved back to the window and stared out. "It's sure a gully washer here."

Jeffrey moved to the front of the store and stood at the open door, watching the rain pound the driveway around the store into mud.

"Yes, now that you mention it, it is strange that this fierce a storm is so localized."

The word "strange" made Jeffrey think of Rebecca and her swiftly changing moods. His whole life had been strange lately. And Rebecca was at the center of the tumult.

She was more than beautiful, with her luminous shiny, red lips, and clouds of dark hair. But he'd never known a girl so unpredictable, so moody, and so hard to understand. She always kept him off center. He never felt in control of his own emotions.

At times he wanted to turn and walk away from her, to never look back. Other times, he felt he never wanted anyone else in his life, no matter how many storms he had to weather.

"Makes life interesting, though, don't it?"

Jeffrey was startled to remember he wasn't alone. The old man had walked up quietly to stand beside him. And read his mind?

"What? Who?"

"The sudden storm. Weather never gets boring out here, so near the ocean."

"Oh, sure. Not boring."

Rebecca was anything but boring.

Chapter 5

By the time Miranda pulled up in front of the small grocery and filling station in her blue Camaro, the storm was over. She could see from the mud and the puddles that there had been a lot of rain. Strange that it skirted Winthrop entirely.

Jeffrey saw her and hurried out. She didn't even have to honk. He looked really glad to see her, and she wondered how he'd gotten stranded in the first place.

"No ride, Jeffrey, until I hear how you got stranded." Miranda started talking the minute he got in the car. She watched him take a deep breath and roll his blue eyes.

"Okay, okay, the truth. Rebecca and I had a fight, or something — "

"How can you have a fight or *something*?" Miranda asked. She backed up her car and turned around.

"She got mad at me and I don't even know why. Something was bothering her, but she wouldn't tell me what it was." Jeffrey stared out the window as they started back to town. He sounded pretty stressed.

Miranda tapped her fingers on the steering wheel and thought about what to do — if she should do anything. This wasn't really her business, even though Jeffrey was her friend and had involved her by calling for help. She drove slowly and let him stew awhile.

"Hey, you missed the road to town." Jeffrey turned to her. At least he noticed.

"You hungry? I'm starved. I have a great idea. We'll stop at Sharkey's and you buy me a hamburger in return for the ride."

"I'm not hungry."

"You will be when you smell the burgers. You need to talk to someone, Jeffrey, and I'm a good listener." Miranda turned into the restaurant's parking lot and found a space easily since it was early for the dinner crowd.

Eyebrows raised when Jeffrey and Miranda came in together, but Miranda didn't care if she was starting some gossip. Everyone she cared about knew that Paul and she were good friends of Barbara and Jeffrey. It was no big deal for her to be with him without Paul along.

Vicki Rorsch was the gossip to squelch. "Hi,

Vicki," said Miranda. "Great storm, wasn't it?" Miranda waved at Vicki and her friends as she passed their table, but she took a seat far away.

"They must live here," Miranda said, sitting down and grabbing a menu. She always ordered the same thing, but she liked to look at the menu first to make sure.

Miranda kept talking without saying anything until their burgers and fries came. After a squirt of catsup and a smear of mustard, Jeffrey picked his burger up and bit into it, forgetting he wasn't hungry. Miranda picked up a fry, dipped it in catsup, and pointed it at Jeffrey before it went into her mouth.

"Okay, shoot. A lot more than Rebecca's pouting spell is bothering you. I pledge never to reveal anything you say to me today." She raised her right hand in a swearing-in motion, then picked up her own burger.

Jeffrey took another bite, sipped his Coke, then spoke in a low voice. "Miranda, getting involved with Rebecca Webster wasn't in my plans. But it's like I can't *not* see her. You know I loved Barbara and I loved her for a long time. We would probably have gotten married some day if — if — "

"If Rebecca Webster hadn't come into town." Miranda guessed that Jeffrey wasn't planning to say if Barbara hadn't died.

Jeffrey closed his eyes and took a deep breath. "Right."

"You were planning to break up with Barbara, weren't you?"

Jeffrey sighed. "I probably would have."

Miranda shook her head and put down her burger. She leaned back and stared at Jeffrey. "I find that hard to believe. After all those years."

"Maybe that was the reason, Miranda. Maybe I didn't really love Barbara as much as I thought I did. I was just used to her. She was comfortable to be with."

"I'm glad Barbara isn't here to hear you say that, Jeffrey. It would break her heart."

"I know. I feel awful about this, Miranda. But I can't seem to help the way I feel, the way I felt even before Barbara had that — that accident. I'm in love with Rebecca Webster."

"You're *possessed* by Rebecca Webster." Miranda's voice hardened. She tried to keep her temper. She didn't want to be Jeffrey's judge and jury, but it was hard not to. She had loved Barbara Matthew like a sister.

"Possession is a good way to put it, Miranda. Rebecca is such a strange person. I've never known anyone like her. I don't think I *want* to be in love with her. But I can't seem to help myself."

"Have you tried?" Tears sprang to Miranda's eyes. She took another bite of her sandwich and almost choked before she could swallow it. The burger was sawdust, the bun cardboard. She pushed her plate back and forced a swallow of her Coke down to clear her throat.

"Yes, I have." Jeffrey pushed his plate aside, too. "You probably won't believe this, but I have tried not to see Rebecca, not to think about her, not to care what happens to her. Nothing works. I find myself calling her, seeking her out."

"And she's always available. Jeffrey, Rebecca Webster is a black widow spider sitting in her web, waiting for you to get close."

"That's a terrible way to describe her, Miranda. A terrible thing to say."

"But I'm right. You may not want to hear me say it, but you know I'm right. Jeffrey, listen to me." Miranda reached out and took both of Jeffrey's hands in hers. She squeezed them, trying to get Jeffrey to come to his senses. She took a deep breath and lowered her voice, but her words were like daggers heading for Jeffrey's chest.

"Jeffrey, don't you see what you're doing? Don't you hear what you're saying? You're sitting here telling me you're in love with the woman who killed Barbara."

Jeffrey jerked his hands back and put them palm out as if to ward off Miranda's words. *"That's not true, Miranda. There's no evidence, not a shred of truth to that.* Rebecca did *not* kill Barbara, and you know it."

"I don't know that. I think just the opposite. There may not be any evidence, there may not be any proof, but I know it as sure as we're sitting here arguing about it. *Rebecca Webster killed Barbara.* She was jealous. She wanted you, and she was having a hard time luring you away from Barbara. She decided the easiest thing to do was get Barbara out of the way. She found her opportunity that day on the boat in a storm, and she took it. I know she said she wasn't on the boat, but *she was.* Somehow she was!"

Miranda was halfway out of her chair, leaning on the table toward Jeffrey. She forced herself to sit down and calm down. She let Jeffrey think about what she'd said. She kept silent for as long as possible.

"Barbara had those marks on her throat, Jeffrey, like someone had choked her. Maybe like a rope burn. What caused that?"

Jeffrey had an explanation on the tip of his tongue, as if he'd thought it all out many times. "Maybe when she fell overboard, she got tangled in the ropes from the boat. Maybe she grabbed at a rope, then the waves tossed the boat about so much she got tangled in the very rope she'd grabbed onto to try and save her life."

Miranda didn't say anything to make Jeffrey feel better about his reasoning. His theory was really far-fetched.

"Maybe someone twisted a rope around her neck, choked her to death, and then tossed her overboard," Miranda said.

Jeffrey's face contorted with pain. "The police still think I did that, even though they don't question me anymore. They just can't prove anything."

"I know you couldn't do that to Barbara, Jeffrey." Miranda's voice softened again. She knew Jeffrey was miserable. As frustrated as she was with his saying he was falling in love with Rebecca, she knew he was also grieving over Barbara. She knew he felt terrible about all of this . . . and confused.

"Miranda, I don't know why she did it, but Rebecca showed me why she wears that ribbon around her neck. There's a terrible scar there like someone had tried to choke her at some time."

"Really? That's curious."

"Whatever happened, she's still terribly angry about it," Jeffrey said.

Miranda didn't know what else to say to Jeffrey. "Let's go home. I think we both need some space; some time to think about all of this. Maybe Rebecca did you a favor, getting angry with you. She's given you some time off. Go home and get some sleep. Try not to do anything stupid."

Jeffrey tossed a tip on the table. "Thanks for your vote of confidence, Miranda. You're a real pal," he said sarcastically.

"I came and rescued you, didn't I?" Miranda headed for the car, leaving Jeffrey to pay their bill. She needed to be alone. The last thing she had wanted to hear from Jeffrey was that he was in love with Rebecca.

In the car, waiting for him, Miranda made a decision. No one seemed to know anything about this girl who had suddenly and mysteriously shown up in Winthrop. There must be some clues that would lead to her past. She couldn't have just appeared out of the fog.

She was going to do some checking. She would trace Rebecca's license plates, or somehow get her driver's license and trace that. Find out where she had come from. Where she had lived before this.

The police, even without proof, still thought that Jeffrey was the guilty person. That Barbara had been killed and it hadn't been an accident. They wouldn't investigate Rebecca Webster.

Miranda could and she would.

Chapter 6

The next day was clear and warm, a day Miranda felt should be devoted to going to the beach, sailing, or lobstering — anything but what she was planning to do.

She wished she had asked Paul to help her. But she knew he would laugh at her or tell Jeffrey. Men tended to think alike and stick together. Now Barbara — Barbara would have loved going along.

Miranda brushed the tears from her cheeks and hurried out to her car. She realized she'd never before felt lonely, and now she missed Barbara so much she could hardly stand getting up in the morning, remembering she was gone. Often she'd get excited about telling Barbara something, sharing something with her, and then she'd remember, she could never share with Barbara again. They could never gossip and laugh or shop and giggle over how a dress or hat looked.

Why didn't Jeffrey feel the same way? Didn't he miss Barbara at all? How could he go on with his life as though nothing had happened?

It was possible that he did feel lonely, that he did miss Barbara, and that he was filling the time and the empty place in his heart with Rebecca. Rebecca was certainly available. More than available. She was obviously after Jeffrey.

Well, Rebecca, watch out. I'm after you.

Miranda pulled off the highway onto the mountain road that led through the woods and up to the old Branford place. The minute the thick, dark stand of evergreens closed around her, she felt vulnerable, alone . . . so alone.

The sun was still low in the east, but even when it was overhead not much light would spill onto this road. Shadows loomed on both sides of her. She slowed the Camaro to a crawl. There was nothing at the end of the road but the Branford house, the cliffs, and the old cemetery. Not another car was on the road.

What was Rebecca Webster doing living out here by herself? Was someone truly coming soon to restore the old house?

Not wanting Rebecca to think this was a social visit, Miranda spotted an old dirt road about half a mile from the Branford place. She pulled off far enough that the Camaro wouldn't be seen from the cliff highway. Locking the car, she placed her keys in her pocket and set out on foot through the woods.

Rebecca's convertible stood out as the one bright spot in the gray landscape of the Branford place. Parked near the back door, the candy-apple-red car contrasted with the weathered gray exterior of the house. No paint was left to peel, and all the boards gleamed like polished pewter, picking up the light where a shaft of sun slid through the trees into the clearing.

Miranda realized that Jeffrey's car was gone. He must have had someone bring him out here really early to get it. Maybe Paul before he went to look for work. Every day Paul went looking, panicked because their summer job had folded when Mr. Smeal turned weird on them.

Two upstairs windows in the house peered at Miranda like dark eyes, watching her approach. But Miranda saw no sign of life. Only one window had a shutter left, and it hung precariously by one hinge. The next hurricane would take it sailing. But the house had stood for a long time, and still had life left in it if someone did decide to restore it. Someone who loved isolation, a desolate landscape, the rhythmic splash of waves on the rocks below the cliffs.

Miranda listened to the ocean slosh against the cliff, whisper as it retreated, roar in again. It should have been a meditative sound. It was a sound she loved when she went to the beach to swim or look for shells after a storm, but now it was menacing.

Barbara had loved to go shelling. They hardly had to call each other, knowing the times to go, the mornings when they'd find the ocean's treasures, tossed up by autumn and winter storms. Often Barbara would show up at Miranda's before school. "Girl, you're crazy," Miranda would say. Barbara would answer, "Let's go. Who cares if we're late?"

As Miranda moved close enough to the house to peer into the first-story windows, the sun disappeared. Fog gathered like a wall of clouds and began to close in.

She went right up to the windows and looked inside. Each room was as it had been before. Empty, coated with dust and cobwebs — no furniture, no sign of life on the first floor at all. Where was Rebecca sleeping?

No way was Miranda going inside. Satisfied

that no family had arrived, and that Rebecca wasn't cleaning up or attempting to get ready for her family, Miranda turned to walk the grounds.

First, she took out a pen and a small notepad she'd stuck in her shirt pocket. She copied down the vanity license plate letters — BEKKA — and noted that it was a Massachusetts plate with a current date.

She longed to get inside the car and search through the glove compartment, but she didn't dare. Rebecca must be around someplace, since her car was here. Miranda knew she could make up an excuse for being here if she was outside, but if she was in the car, snooping, that would be pretty obvious.

A slight noise swung Miranda around. She crouched behind the car and peeked out in the direction of what sounded like a door opening and closing.

It was. Rebecca came out of the old house, dressed in a long black nightgown. Her dark hair floated behind her. She looked neither right nor left, but walked forward silently. She passed right in front of the convertible, moving toward the back of the house and the cliffs. Miranda followed, hiding behind one tree, then another.

The fog was thicker now, helping to hide

her, but soon it hid Rebecca as well. Just before she got to the cliffs, Rebecca turned and walked to her right. Miranda knew if she went far enough she'd come to the old cemetery.

Counting on that to be Rebecca's destination, Miranda decided to catch up with her later. Right now, she had a chance to go inside the house and she was going to take it.

The front door wasn't locked, but it creaked terribly when Miranda opened it. Had anyone been near, they'd have heard it for sure. Miranda froze in place for a few seconds, looked back outside toward the cemetery. She saw nothing.

Running, her tennis shoes thudding softly, Miranda made a quick search of the bottom floor. The kitchen hadn't been used for years. Where did Rebecca eat? Didn't she ever want a cup of tea at night or a snack? There was a thick layer of dust everywhere, even on the floor.

Satisfied that there was nothing of interest on the first floor, Miranda peered out the windows facing south, then ran up the wide staircase to the second floor. Most of the stairs groaned or creaked, adding to the ghostly atmosphere. But Miranda was committed.

She dashed in and out of room after empty room. There was no one. Nothing. If there had ever been any furniture left here, it had been stolen. Most of the windows were broken or coated with so much dust one could hardly see out.

Finally, in a back bedroom, she came to a room with a cot. Here was where Rebecca slept. In a sleeping bag, on a cot, all alone. There was a small suitcase perched on a straight chair. A pair of black jeans and a T-shirt lay tossed on the chair back. A black tank top sprawled like a sleeping cat on the floor.

Miranda stepped closer. A hairbrush lay on a pillow, long strands of black hair trailing from the bristles. She saw no toiletries, no makeup kit, no food. But then, Rebecca's skin was so perfect, she didn't need makeup.

All of a sudden, Miranda couldn't stay in the house a minute longer. There was a melancholy feeling here, a heavy dark atmosphere that was hard to fight off. Miranda felt cold . . . and frightened.

She turned, fully expecting to see Rebecca standing, watching her. When she wasn't, Miranda fled, pounding down the staircase, not caring how much noise she made.

Outside, the fog was even thicker, but Miranda didn't feel quite so trapped. She headed in the direction that Rebecca had taken, determined to find out where the mysterious girl was walking, barefoot and in her black nightgown.

She tried not to make any noise, slipping from tree to tree. Dead leaves, dampened by the recent rain, lay like a soft, thick carpet, muffling her footsteps. Fog curls floated in and out between dark tree trunks. Occasionally the fog lifted; more often it presented a solid wall of gray clouds.

Just in time, a slight breeze cleared the path under her feet. Miranda slowed, peering ahead, stopping often to listen.

What she heard surprised her. Someone was crying.

She slipped closer and stopped behind a giant oak tree. Ahead were a number of graves, marked with silver-gray stones like rows of rotting fence boards. A few stones had tumbled to the ground. Occasionally one lay flat like a small gray coffin above the earth.

Rebecca, in her billowing black gown, hair falling down her back, stood before a marker, smaller than most, suggesting the grave of a child. Who could be buried there?

Miranda couldn't see Rebecca's face, but she could never mistake the sound of quiet weeping.

Chapter 7

I faint when my jailers open the door to my tiny closet cell. I wake to find myself back in the cell with Mercy and her daughter, Dorcas. This cell seems enormous to my eyes as I look around in disbelief at my luck.

Luck! I despair to think myself lucky for having only a larger cell.

Mercy kneels beside me, one cool hand on my cheek, the other holding my hands where they rest over my stomach.

"You poor child. I have thought of nothing but you for days."

"Why am I here? Where is Goody Lyman?"

"Her husband found the money to buy her freedom. They hurried her trial, and, of course, with enough pay for the judge, she was found innocent."

I groan and turn my face to the wall. The

hay in the mattress rustles and pricks my skin, but I relish how good it feels to stretch out, to lie prone instead of crouched in a heap over my feet.

"Rebecca, I have been lucky, too. My poor Silas was able to sell off a parcel of our land. He gave money for me to have food and tea and enough water to bathe. I have saved the bathwater, not knowing when I will get more. I want you to use it. Clean yourself up. You will feel better. And when you are ready, I'll make you a cup of hot tea. Look, I have sugar. I will even light a small fire. You can wash your hair if you like. This soap is foul-smelling, but I can't tell you what clean hair has done for Dorcas and me."

I find tears in my eyes again at Mercy's kindness. How can anyone accuse this kind woman of being a witch? And her daughter, her sweet daughter, Dorcas, is so innocent. She watches me, blond hair like a halo around her face, blue eyes huge, wondering, I'm sure, where I have been.

I strip little by little and wash, hating the smell of the soap, loving the way clean skin bristles in the cold. I rub down the goose bumps with my cloak, having no other towel.

I wash my hair and Mercy patiently combs it

until she gets out the snarls and tangles. I love the feel of it tickling my bare shoulders. I lean back and laugh, actually laugh.

"You feel better, don't you? I knew you would. Now for a cup of tea, real tea. Bless Silas. I know it pained him to sell our land. He worked so hard to buy acre after acre when we came here. But he says that without me there, nothing seems to matter. He is confident that my trial will be soon and that I will be declared innocent."

Mercy prepares me a cup of steaming tea and adds a heaping spoon of sugar. She has such a meager supply, but she is generous beyond belief. I know I would want to hoard every leaf of tea and every tiny crystal of sugar.

I cup my hands around the cracked bowl from which I drink, feeling better than I have for a long time. I, too, have hope that this nightmare will soon be over.

But it has just begun.

The next day they come for Mercy and Dorcas. It is time for Mercy's trial. When she returns, her face is pale, her eyes smudged into her face and red with her crying.

I cradle her in my arms when they shove her back into the cell. "What verdict, Mercy? What has happened?"

"Guilty, I am declared guilty, Rebecca. And

tomorrow — tomorrow I am to be hanged. Why not today? Oh, why didn't they take me out there and do it now? I cannot stand to think about dying."

I sit, stunned at the news. Finally I say, "And Dorcas?"

"Guilty, too. They say the daughter of a witch is sure to have been stained with her sin. They say I have had time to teach her all my spells and wicked ways." Mercy starts to cry almost uncontrollably. "Oh, Rebecca, how can such a small, innocent child be declared a witch? They are mad. They are all mad. Women I thought to be my friends testified against me. They told of unmentionable deeds, awful spells I put on them, their men, and their animals."

"They are afraid, Mercy, terribly afraid."

What else can I say? I, too, know our world has gone mad. And I know that if Mercy is declared guilty, I have no chance to escape the same sentence. It is only a matter of time.

When they come for Mercy, I beg them to leave the child, Dorcas, with me. Mercy begs me to keep her safe.

"She needs to see what happens to witches. This will be a lesson to her to see her mother hanged for her evil deeds." The jailers delight in the evil they are doing.

"But if she is to suffer the same penalty," I

argue, "why should she see this today? Do you murder her today as well?"

I have put all my anger into my last words and am penalized for speaking out. One guard slaps my face until my ears ring. I fall to the floor, soaking my skirts in the rancid, standing water.

Dorcas clings to her mother's skirts and both are dragged from the cell. I throw myself on my straw, but have no tears left. I cannot cry.

In what seems like a very short time, Dorcas is returned to me. Her face is pale and her eyes huge. She stares into space as if she is struck deaf and dumb. How can a four-year-old endure what she has seen? Perhaps she has lost her mind. This would be for the best. I hope this for her. She will not remember seeing her mother choke and spin at the end of a rope. She will feel nothing when they do the same to her.

I cradle her in my arms and rock and rock her as if she is a newborn. Her body is warm in mine, but so tiny, so frail. So helpless to stand up to this insanity.

Neither of us cries. Neither of us thinks into the future.

A cold wind brought Rebecca back to the present. She didn't know how long she had been staring at the small gray gravestone that read "Dorcas Smith. Born 1688. Died 1692. Hanged as a witch four days following her mother, Mercy Smith. An angel in both this life and the next."

Taking a deep breath, Rebecca sensed she was not alone. She spun around and spotted Miranda watching her. The anger she felt at Dorcas's fate was transferred to Miranda.

"What are *you* doing here?"

"I — I — " Miranda seemed startled to have Rebecca discover her. "I came to talk to you."

"I have nothing to say. You're on my land. Get off."

"Rebecca, I want to talk to you about Jeffrey."

"Stay out of Jeffrey's life. And mine. You have no business interfering with us. What he does is up to him. And what I do is certainly none of your concern."

"But it is. Jeffrey is unhappy, and he is a friend of mine."

"Jeffrey unhappy?" Rebecca threw back her head and laughed heartily. "Jeffrey is anything but unhappy. Confused, perhaps. But men are easily confused. He loves me."

"He does not love you. He loved Barbara. He is fascinated by you. He is vulnerable right now because of Barbara's death. You're taking advantage of that. You're casting some kind of spell with no concern for him. If you care for him at all, you'll let him go."

"Let him go? He's a big boy. He can go if he likes. Ask him. Ask him what *he* wants to do. If he wants to walk away from me, he can. You seem to think I have some magic powers, that I can hold him against his will. Go. Talk to him."

"I have. I have talked to him, Rebecca. He thinks you killed Barbara," Miranda lied. "He's trying to get you to confess, or to slip up and say you killed Barbara. That's why he's hanging around you."

Rebecca laughed again, knowing Miranda was lying. "That's not true, Miranda, and you know it isn't true. Jeffrey knows that Barbara's death was an accident."

"*I* know you killed her." Miranda's face twisted in pain, making Rebecca know she was right. Jeffrey had never said he suspected Rebecca.

"You *know* I killed Barbara? What proof do you have? Why would I do such a thing?" Rebecca smiled and ran her red-tipped fingers through her dark hair.

"To get Jeffrey. You knew you didn't have a chance while Barbara was alive. They were too close. They had been together too long.

You are evil, Rebecca Webster. And I plan to find proof."

Rebecca saw Miranda step back and took advantage of her losing her nerve.

"If I am evil, Miranda, if I'm a killer, then I may not hesitate to kill again. You're up here, all alone with me. Doesn't that make you just a little bit nervous? I'm sure no one knows where you are. That you came here all on your own, all by yourself to spy on me."

Rebecca took a step toward Miranda.

Miranda stepped back, one hand behind her to keep from backing into a tree. Reaching, reaching for something with which to defend herself should Rebecca attack. Reading Miranda's mind was so easy that Rebecca had to laugh.

Her voice rose and fell with laughter, delighted laughter.

Miranda turned and dashed away through the woods.

Chapter 8

Miranda ran until she was back at her car. She didn't know how she made it — she was a tennis player, not a runner. But suddenly she had been terribly afraid. What Rebecca had said made sense. If she had killed Barbara, what was to stop her killing again? She had guessed right, too; Miranda had told no one where she was going. She would be a fool to underestimate Rebecca.

She bent over double to try to relieve the pain in her side, to catch her breath. Her stomach heaved and she felt as if she might throw up.

Her dizziness passed, and she started to breathe normally, to gain control of her nerves and her senses. Now what? What good had it done to come up here? She hadn't even seen whose grave Rebecca stood in front of, whose grave had caused her to cry. Miranda thought it would take a lot to get Rebecca to stand in the damp and cold, crying. But she certainly wasn't going back up there right now to find out the name on that small headstone.

The only information Miranda had gained from her scouting expedition was that Rebecca was staying in that old house alone, and that there were no signs that her family would arrive at any minute.

Miranda tried to think of circumstances that would bring her to do the same. She could think of nothing.

Miranda got back in her Camaro and started the engine. She was glad to leave the mountaintop. Fog swirled; thick humid clouds closed around her. She'd have to drive about two miles an hour to be sure to stay on the road. It was going to take her forever to get home.

For a few moments after Miranda left, Rebecca stood in the graveyard and thought about the girl coming up here alone. That took courage. And loyalty. Miranda had been Barbara's best friend, so that meant she was good friends with Jeffrey, too. And she was being loyal to them both. Rebecca admired loyalty in a person.

Loyalty was a difficult thing for Rebecca to think about. It was loyalty that had been her downfall.

"Rebecca, you mustn't. You mustn't try to defend me. You have to stay as far away from me as possible. Pretend you never even knew me." Sarah holds both of Rebecca's hands and her eyes plead with Rebecca, her best friend.

"I can't do that, Sarah," I say, hugging Sarah tightly. "You know I can't. You are my best friend. I can't pretend I don't know you. Everyone would know I was lying. Everyone knows we are as close as sisters, perhaps closer. I will testify for you."

"Oh, Rebecca, I'm so frightened. For you and for me. What will happen to us?"

"They will question you and see they are wrong. You can't possibly be a witch. They will listen to me and your other friends and they'll know they made a mistake."

Sarah keeps shaking her head back and forth in disbelief. How can anyone accuse her of witchcraft in the first place? They say her mother, who has just last month died of the pox, was a witch and her getting smallpox was the proof. Their reason for arresting Sarah is that daughters of witches almost always are witches, too. Mothers don't want their knowledge to die with them, so they pass it on to the most likely person, the oldest daughter.

"Oh, Rebecca, if you even try to testify for me, you will lose your temper. You know how easily it gets away from you. You will say things that will make the judge angry. You will get yourself in trouble. I know you will. Please, please don't do this. I beg you, stay home, hide, run away. Get away from this place where these awful things are happening."

Thinking back, Rebecca knew Sarah was right. She should have left Salem, she should have run away. Her mother was afraid for her. She wanted to send Rebecca to her cousin who lived in New York. But Rebecca was stubborn. She wouldn't leave. And she did testify for Sarah.

She did lose her temper at the trial. And she made the judge very angry. So angry that only five days later, she found herself in prison. Men had come to her door. They had arrested her, and carried her to the jail, screaming and kicking. Her mother screamed and cried. Her father swore and called out to Rebecca to go quietly. He'd get her out in no time.

But he hadn't. Her parents hadn't even had enough money to make her comfortable while she was there. Waiting.

Rebecca brushed tears from her cheeks, turned, and ran all the way back to the old house where she was staying.

Quickly, she dressed. Memories were good things. Memories were what she needed more of. She had to remember what she was doing here. She had to remember *why* she had returned.

She ran for her car to go to town. She must find Jeffrey and apologize.

She must make him love her with all his heart and soul and mind. He had to be fully in her power.

She had power. She knew she could accomplish what she had set out to do. It was just taking longer than she'd thought.

But what did that matter? The one thing Rebecca had plenty of was time.

Chapter 9

During the drive to town, Rebecca worked out carefully what she would do. It was hard for her to think up jobs to do around the old house she was living in, but that was the only way she knew to get Jeffrey to come.

Six-year-old Tony let her in when she rang the Thomases' doorbell. "Hi, Rebecca." Tony grabbed her hand. "Jeff just got up. He's eating breakfast. Want some?"

"No, I ate a long time ago, Tony. But I'll come watch Jeffrey eat. How about you?"

"I ate hours ago, too. I guess we're both early birds. Jeff would sleep till noon if Mom let him."

Rebecca laughed. Tony made her feel almost alive and almost happy.

Jeffrey's brown hair was still sleep tousled, and he yawned as Tony and Rebecca came into the kitchen. Then he saw who was with

Tony. "Rebecca! What are you doing here so early?" He ran his hands through his hair to comb it. Embarrassment showed in his beautiful blue eyes.

"Can I come out to your house today, Rebecca?" Tony sat at the table and took a piece of toast from Jeffrey's plate. He smeared it with strawberry jam and stuffed half of it in his mouth.

"Tony — "

"Sure you can, Tony. I was going to ask Jeffrey to work today. Maybe you can help us. We can go swimming after we get some work done. Does that sound like a good plan?" Rebecca held out her hand.

"Right on." Tony jumped up and slapped Rebecca's palm in a high five. "Oops, sorry." He left a smear of jam on Rebecca's fingers.

She put them in her mouth. "I love strawberry jam. I used to make wild strawberry jam every summer." Rebecca's eyes were shadowed with memories.

"Would you like some breakfast, Rebecca?" Jeffery asked, unable to take his eyes from Rebecca's.

"No, thanks." Rebecca held Jeffrey's eyes with an intense look, making him look away first.

"Why don't you go get your bathing suit, Tony, and your swim fins," Rebecca suggested.

Tony ran off to his room. Rebecca watched him go, putting off looking at Jeffrey again.

"I'm sorry, Jeffrey, for losing my temper, for acting so unreasonable. And I *do* need help at the house. Please." She never took her eyes from Jeffrey's.

Unable to resist, Jeffrey said, "Rebecca, I'll come out and work, but I'm taking Mom's car. Something seems to be wrong with mine, and she left hers for me today." Jeffrey went back to eating.

"I'm sorry I left you to get yourself home yesterday, Jeffrey, but I didn't dream your car wouldn't start. Please forgive me. I wasn't really mad at you. I had something else on my mind." Rebecca made her voice soft and appealing.

"I'm still taking a car." Jeffrey stared at his plate.

"I promise I'll bring you home. That's a waste of gas to take two cars. Tony will be along. I'd never make both of you walk home." She smiled again and placed her hand on Jeffrey's arm. Her lips were slightly parted. Her eyes soft.

"I'm not sure about Tony going with us," Jeffrey said, aware of her hand on his arm with every nerve in his body.

"Why not? We won't let him swim until we're with him. He can work. I'll pay both of you."

Jeffrey pulled his arm away from Rebecca and got up to rinse his dishes.

"Jeffrey, I know you hate working for me, but you need a job, and I need help. Money is no problem. Think about how much it's going to cost to go to school next fall. Swallow your pride and pretend that I'm an old cranky lady." Rebecca got up to stand next to Jeffrey. She circled his shoulders with her arm. She could feel his muscles tense through his T-shirt.

Jeffrey turned to her. "You may not be old, but you're sure hard to predict, Rebecca. I don't like your suddenly being angry when I haven't done anything wrong. I don't like thinking I have to be careful around you or you'll be moody."

Jeffrey succumbed to her arm around him. He turned and took Rebecca in his arms. She tipped her head back and looked at him. "I promise to reform. I promise to be Miss Nice."

"Well, not too nice." He kissed her warmly. She felt her blood move like liquid fire through her body.

Tony interrupted them. "If you're going to do that all day, I'm not going after all. I don't like that barfy love stuff." He tossed his backpack on the kitchen table and reached for the last piece of toast on a plate in the center.

"It's going to be hard to please both of you." Rebecca stepped away from Jeffrey, but kept her eyes on his. The look she saw there almost frightened her. Getting Jeffrey to fall in love with her was too easy. Keeping her own feelings under control was harder. "Come on, Tony. Let's wait in the car for your brother."

When Jeffrey came out to get in the car, Tony was firmly settled in the front passenger seat, and Rebecca was drumming her long fingers with their bright red nails on the steering wheel. Jeffrey tossed his gear into the convertible, stepped over into the backseat, and said, "Let's go to work."

Rebecca let Tony turn the radio to his favorite rock station and pulled out of the driveway. She felt she could drive this car forever. Tipping her head back, she let the wind blow through her black hair, let it clear her mind, freshen her resolve.

They started up the mountain, and Rebecca slowed a little so Jeffrey wouldn't worry about her driving. She always drove too fast, racing to get somewhere. Sometimes for reasons she didn't understand.

The morning fog had burned off and the day sparkled, clean and clear. Rebecca found she was glad to be here. Maybe it was all right if things took longer than she'd thought.

Time was of no concern to her. She looked at Jeffrey in the rearview mirror. He smiled. She smiled back, and her anticipation for the day grew almost beyond her patience.

She closed her eyes for a second. Slow and easy, slow and easy. Today belonged to her. She'd let nothing spoil this one day.

Chapter 10

They worked, clearing brush from the back of the old house until almost noon. Even Tony worked hard, which surprised Rebecca.

"I feel as if I have two men working for me," she said once and Tony smiled.

"You do! I can do a man's work, can't I, Jeff?" Tony raised his right arm and made a muscle. "I'm strong."

"You're Super Brother." Jeffrey looked up at Tony and smiled. Rebecca could see that Jeffrey, no matter how much they teased, was crazy about Tony. That could come in handy, she realized, if she needed to use it. Maybe she wouldn't. She cared about Tony, herself, more than she wanted to admit. She had always wished she'd had a brother or sister, but it hadn't happened.

"Well, I'd better find something to eat for you two." Rebecca realized she didn't have one bite in the house. Not a can or a box or a bottle of anything. Not even any soft drinks or lemonade. "You two keep working. I'll scare up something."

"Scare up something?" Tony asked, wrinkling his nose. "Like a rabbit for stew?"

Rebecca looked surprised. She knew how to prepare a rabbit stew. "Is that what you want?"

"I'd rather have pizza." Tony leaned on his rake.

"Don't come until I call you, and I'll have a surprise." Rebecca flew into the house and grabbed her car keys.

She let the red convertible coast until she was a short distance from the house, then started the engine. She drove the way she liked to drive down the mountain and screeched to a halt in front of Gino's Pizza.

Three men standing on the street turned to look at her when she got out of the car. She smiled at them and loved the startled look on their faces. One whistled, one smiled, the other tipped his cap to her. Oh, she loved the effect she had on men. She had never been able to do this before, and it was exciting. It made her heart beat faster. She had had to pretend she was modest and shy and quiet. She'd had to wear awful dresses with no style, to hide her body. All the women around her did the same, and some seemed to like that life, but she had always hated it, hated the pretending.

She especially loved the power she had here. Power was something she wasn't sure she had before. Now she knew she had all she needed.

"One large pizza with 'everything.' " Rebecca read from the big board behind the counter. "And could you hurry?" She gave her most persuasive smile to the boy behind the counter. He could hardly take his eyes off her to get to work.

"Sure. It's our busy time but — "

Rebecca waved a five dollar bill at him, clutching it with her long fingernails so he had to touch her to take it. "For your trouble." She knew money would tempt him. Money had a lot of power over these people.

"Sure. You can have the next one I make." He glanced up to see if anyone in the restaurant had heard him say that, had seen him take the tip. Then he pulled a pan lined with dough toward him and went to work.

Going back up the mountain, the pizza smelled strong. Rebecca wondered how it would taste.

"Lunch," she called out the door as soon as she had carried the box inside and opened it. She found two cracked plates in the back of the cupboard.

She probably should have taken the food outside, she realized, looking at the layer of dust on the kitchen counters.

Scooping up the pizza box, she hurried back outside and set it on the back steps. The wood in the steps was worn and splintery, but sturdy.

She had bought a bottle of Coke and one of 7-UP, not knowing what Tony liked to drink. Jeffrey liked Coke; she knew that from being with him in town.

Tony skipped by her to the bathroom. "I have to wash my hands," he called back. "Don't eat it all before I get back."

"He's crazy about you," Jeffrey said, walking up to the steps. He stared at Rebecca as if he was trying to figure out something or read her mind. Her black shorts and tank top clung to her body. "You don't look as if you worked one minute this morning," he said.

Jeffrey had his shirt off and his chest was shining with sweat. His hair had curled slightly with the heat and dampness of perspiration.

"I didn't work much," Rebecca confessed.

"I'd better wash up, too. A swim is going to feel great."

Tony came outside and Jeffrey went in. Rebecca smiled at Tony. "Help yourself."

Tony took a slice of pizza and stuffed the point in his mouth. After he'd chewed and swallowed, he said, "Your house is sure dirty. Aren't you supposed to have it cleaned up by the time your family gets here?"

Rebecca took a deep breath and looked away. "They won't mind."

Jeffrey came outside and sat on the second step from the top.

"When is your family coming? You haven't made much progress inside."

"It's rather hopeless. Maybe I'll wait and let them help me. I confess, I'm rather lazy." Rebecca folded her legs and sat in the grass that Jeffrey had mowed the last time he'd worked for her.

They ate without talking much. Jeffrey and Tony were so hungry they didn't notice that Rebecca only pretended to eat the pizza.

After lunch they headed down the cliffs to the ocean. Jeffrey felt they should work some more, but Rebecca insisted they play for awhile. She couldn't tell Jeffrey she didn't care if the yard work ever got done.

The day was hot, as hot as it had been for weeks. Rebecca didn't swim at all. She lay on a towel in her black bathing suit and watched Jeffrey play with Tony.

Tony finally settled down to combing the tide pools for crabs.

And Jeffrey sat on a towel next to Rebecca.

Rebecca said, digging in her swim bag, "Will you put some suntan lotion on my back?"

"Sure." Jeffrey poured lotion from the bottle Rebecca handed him and rubbed it in with long slow strokes.

Rebecca arched her back and enjoyed the feel of his fingers on her skin. "If I was a cat I'd purr."

"And I'd watch for your claws."

"You don't trust me, do you?" She turned and looked into his eyes.

"It's hard to. I just don't understand you," Jeffrey said. His hand left her back and moved to her shoulders. He lingered on one arm, then the other, gently massaging. His touch was a caress that had Rebecca spinning down and down as if a deep ocean whirlpool twisted and turned her, sucked her under. Finally he gripped one arm and turned her around.

His lips found hers and he kissed her deeply. She let herself go, kissed him back, her fingers gripping both his arms, then circling his back, pulling him even closer.

Finally he pulled away, breathing deeply. She ducked her head and buried it in his chest. He smelled of sun and sea. She felt his heart pounding rapidly as he breathed. She knew she excited him, that he was in love with her. That now he held back, trying to stay in control of his own emotions.

She played with fire, since her own emotions were on edge. It wasn't going to take much more for her to be wildly swept away by this man. She could so easily forget why she was here. What she had to do.

Taking deep breaths, she let air out slowly, squeezing her eyes tight. Hot tears trickled down her cheeks before she could stop them. A knot swelled inside her chest, rose and rose into her throat, threatening to choke her.

"Rebecca, what's wrong? You're crying. I didn't mean to upset you."

Pulling away from him, she got to her feet quickly. "You would never understand. Not in a million years could I make you understand."

"Try. Please try, Rebecca. Don't shut me out. Please, talk to me. I can help you. I know I can if you'll be honest with me. If you'll tell me what's bothering you."

"No! I can't! Just leave me alone!" She could hardly see as she ran down the sandy beach toward where Tony searched the tide pools.

She whispered, "This isn't fair. It isn't fair!"

Chapter 11

Rebecca sat next to Tony, while he searched the tide pools. She didn't speak. Didn't answer him as he chattered. Finally, after taking a long swim, Jeffrey made his way over to where they were.

"The tide is coming in. I think it would be better to come out now, Tony. The waves crashing on those rocks will be dangerous." Jeffrey waded back into the water and took Tony's hand.

Jeffrey said nothing to Rebecca about her running away from him, and she pretended it had never happened. But soon she took them home. Jeffrey got out of the car without looking at Rebecca and she patted Tony's shoulder.

"Call me if you have more work to be done," Tony said.

"I will." Rebecca didn't look back as she pulled away.

She raced back up the mountain, parked her car in the drive, and walked to the edge of the cliffs, staring out over the ocean. Waves whispered against the rocks below, then splashed louder as the tide brought more and more water toward shore. She listened until the water roared in and sucked out, hissing lacy foam around the rocks.

She sat on the bank, dangling her feet over the grassy cliff. *I cannot, cannot fall in love with Jeffrey Thomas.* She concentrated on reliving the terrible injustice that had started her anger.

I am dragged from my parents' house, my mother crying and screaming. I am too frightened to protest, and since two strong men take both of my arms, it would do little good to try to escape. I look back and carry the memory of my mother's face, twisted with fear and despair.

After two months in prison my spirit is broken and I arrive at my trial dirty and disheveled, looking as if I have lived on the streets for all of this time.

I know ahead of time I am doomed, and at first I listen to the tales of my accusers with lowered head and little fight left.

I listen to Judge Thomas read out my sins.

"Rebecca Webster, you are accused of witch-

craft. We are here today to listen to your testimony and that of your accusers."

"Sarah Hooker has already been tried, found guilty, and hanged as a witch. I have heard testimony that Sarah was your friend and that you testified in her favor, saying she was innocent."

Thinking of what they did to Sarah starts a fire in my chest that lifts my head and straightens my shoulders. "Sarah Hooker was one of the best women I have ever known. She was no witch."

"But she confessed."

"What ways did you torture her to get her to say this for your benefit?" I stare into the eyes of Judge Thomas and he looks back at his book. I shudder to think of what they may have done to Sarah before they tried and killed her.

Judge Thomas was not here to talk about Sarah Hooker, except where it went against me. "I have the testimony of Jack Gove that he found signs on your body, and that his wife found further signs."

I remember Jack Gove tearing off my blouse when they took me to the jail. I blush to recall the pleasure in his eyes as he found and touched the birthmark on my left shoulder. At least he had the decency to let his wife and her sister search the rest of my body for other signs. I do not answer this accusation from the judge as it will do no good.

The people who will testify against me file in. I know they are afraid and will say anything to shift guilt onto me and away from themselves. I try to forgive them in advance and understand their fear. Everyone in town, especially the women, must be terrified by now. No one is safe.

"I saw her playing with three yellow birds in the woods," testifies a child I had thought was my friend. Her eyes are wide and she paints a wild picture. "The birds flew round and round her head, singing. Then they landed on her outstretched hand and she fed them. Each time she went into the woods she could call them back to her. I knew then I was watching a witch at play and I was scared."

"I saw her mix a potion with a dead cat and three goat's eyes. Then she carried this potion to Goody Carter's goats who searched for food in the woods. They drank and all died within two days."

The man who testifies to this is a fool. Halfwitted, he wanders the street begging. I think he has seen me burying my dear cat Tabitha who died of old age. I took her to the woods and had a funeral for her, placing wild flowers and colored rocks on her grave.

What other lies have they gathered against me?

Goody Wilson told of her baby dying soon after I took her a bouquet of wild flowers, which she mistakenly kept in a vase by her bed, not knowing my power.

I cannot look to see if my mother and father are here today. I know if my accusers kill me they will also be killing my mother. Already frail, my fate will be her death blow.

I grow faint from being half starved in the prison. Someone brings a chair for me. Rough hands push me down.

It is hard to listen to so many lies and my mind drifts. Then I get renewed energy when I hear the judge say, "Rebecca Webster, how do you plead to all these accusations? What do you say in your defense?"

I leap to my feet and despite the heavy chains that tear at my hands and my bare feet, I move to where Judge Thomas sits in judgment of me, all powerful, all evil himself.

"I say you are all mad. I am innocent of all this foolishness you have drummed up against me, as was my dear friend Sarah Hooker and her mother who saved many lives in this town, as was Mercy Smith and her child, Dorcas, only four years old. How can a four-year-old child

be anything but innocent? I point one dirty finger with its torn nail at Judge Thomas. "You will rue the day you have sat in this mock court. If I am a witch, and you seem determined to say that I am, I have the power to curse you and all your descendants. And I do so now."

Judge Thomas cannot help but shrink at my last words. He stares at me with disbelief. I keep my eyes steady and full of hatred, staring back. He looks down and shuffles the papers in front of him.

A hush falls over all the courtroom, so many people shocked at my words, shocked that I would dare defy the law and those who sit here in judgment of me.

I think now I am mad, too, since I toss back my head and laugh. I know I will regret my ready temper and my foolish, but satisfying, outburst.

The judge waits until my voice is stilled as is the room. He clears his throat twice before he speaks.

"Rebecca Webster, for the horrible crime of witchcraft of which you are certainly guilty, I sentence you as the law directs. On Tuesday next, being the fifteenth day of August, between the hours of eight and noon, you will be taken to Gallows Hill and hanged by the neck until you are dead."

With a flourish Judge Thomas signs the paper from which he reads. Even though I expect this sentence, even though I have known this to be my fate from the time I was taken prisoner, my insides constrict and churn. I am beset with a terrible dread and fear of my actual death. There is something else he surely cannot know that distresses me further.

On August fifteenth I will be seventeen years of age.

That night, after Jeffrey had eaten dinner, only because his mother watched him and he didn't want to worry her, he stood at the window in his room.

Black clouds had drifted in from the east, swirling around the town of Winthrop, threatening for hours. Thunder rumbled in the distance, then grew closer and closer until loud crashes sent everyone for cover. Lightning split the sky in a terrible display of fireworks.

Even during hurricane season, Jeffrey had never seen such a storm. It was as if all the gods in heaven had unleashed their power in a display of stored-up anger.

Tony burst into the room and ran to stand beside Jeffrey. He hugged Jeffrey.

"I'm scared, Jeff. We never had a storm this bad. Can I sleep with you? Please, can I?"

Tony buried his face in Jeffrey's stomach.

Jeffrey hugged Tony back but didn't speak.

"What's happening, Jeff? What's happening up there? Aren't you scared?"

Jeffrey was surprised to find that he *was* frightened. He had lived on this coast for eighteen years. He had always loved the storms, and sometimes sat in his window seat to watch. But this storm — there was something different about this thunderstorm. He had no idea what, or why he felt that. The idea came from deep inside him. Some long-buried memory, perhaps, or something that had happened in the past that he could not recall.

Some instinct said that this particular storm was more dangerous than any he had ever witnessed. He was glad to let Tony sleep with him. He was glad not to be alone tonight.

He shivered for a long time, fighting off pure gut fear. Something was definitely not right with the world. No — Something was not right with *his* world. For some reason he was absolutely certain that this terrible storm had something to do with his own, already disturbing life.

Chapter 12

The next morning at breakfast, Tony made an announcement. "Jeff loves Rebecca." He stuffed his mouth with blueberry pancakes, then grinned at Jeffrey with blue teeth.

"Is that so?" Mrs. Thomas said. She looked at Jeffrey. "*Is* that so?" The expression on her face said this was neither good nor bad, but she was curious to know the truth.

Jeffrey poured maple syrup on his pancakes. "See if I let you sleep with me again when you're scared to pieces by a little thunder."

"You were scared, Jeff," Tony accused. "I could see that you were scared, too."

"I'd say last night had a lot of thunder." Mrs. Thomas let Jeffrey change the subject. "I don't think I've ever seen a storm like that."

"Me either. Where's Dad?" Jeffrey put the first taste of the sweet breakfast in his mouth, surprised that he was hungry after forcing down dinner last night.

"He's been at the store since dawn. There's been a lot of electrical and house damage." Mrs. Thomas poured Jeffrey a cup of coffee. "He said during the storm he expected a lot of damage this morning. The news said lots of trees were uprooted on the mountain around the cliffs. I hope Rebecca is okay up there by herself."

Jeffrey wondered how long it would take his mother to get back to the subject she wanted to hear about. "I think she can take care of herself," Jeffrey said.

"Well, most women can, but that doesn't mean we shouldn't worry about her. A tree may have come down on that old house or on her car or — "

"Are you saying I should go up there and check on her?" Jeffrey didn't know if he wanted an excuse to do that or not.

His mother shrugged. "That would be a kind thing to do." She still gave him room to wiggle out of talking about how much he liked or disliked Rebecca.

He had always been able to talk to his mother. Of course, he never had a problem like this. Loving Barbara had taken a smooth and even course. Their relationship had been comfortable. He didn't think they'd ever had a fight. Was that good or bad? It was nice.

He didn't feel as if he and Rebecca had had a fight yesterday, but he knew something had gone wrong. Every time he kissed her, she got upset. She had kissed him back. She seemed always to respond to his showing her he was in love with her. But then she'd pull back. Had she been hurt before? Before she came here? By someone only pretending to love her?

Tony finished his breakfast and ran out to check on the storm damage. "I'm going to go see the world."

"Be careful, Tony," Mrs. Thomas called to him. "There are a lot of downed electrical lines."

"I will, Mom. I know that. Dad showed me. I'm not dumb."

Both Mrs. Thomas and Jeffrey laughed, then got very quiet. Finally Jeffrey spoke. "I'm not dumb, either, Mom, but I *am* puzzled."

"Want to talk about it? I've been worried about you, Jeff. I can see what you're going through, and I don't know how to help. Sometimes the timing is off for relationships. You haven't had time to grieve for Barbara, but here comes Rebecca out of the blue, and you know you like her."

"How come you're so smart, Mom?" Jeffrey smiled, and accepted the second cup of coffee his mother poured him. She filled her cup, too, and sat back down opposite him, ready to listen or talk, whatever he needed.

"I've lived a long time."

"You watch soap operas." Jeffrey teased her.

"Does this seem like a soap opera to you, Jeff?"

"Sometimes. I think I was about to break up with Barbara, Mom, and I guess I feel guilty about that. I'm even glad I didn't have to hurt her, but — "

"There are several kinds of love, Jeff, and different intensities. You had known Barbara for a long time, and I'm not saying you didn't love her, but — well, Rebecca is an exciting woman, totally different from Barbara. Could you be caught up in that excitement, that thrill of someone so different?"

"I guess I could. I've thought of that." Jeffrey played with his spoon, stirring and stirring the cream in his coffee to a toffee brown. Then he sipped the drink. "I think what puzzles me most, Mom, is not whether or not I care for Rebecca, but every time I show her I like her, she pulls back. I think she likes me, and often she shows that she does. Then sometimes she gets really mad at me for kissing her."

"This sounds like a woman being careful, a woman who has been badly hurt before. She's afraid."

"What should I do about it?"

"Nothing. Just don't rush things. You have to let her learn to trust you a little at a time."

"Miranda is mad at me. She thinks I'm being disloyal to Barbara. She still thinks that Rebecca might have had something to do with Barbara's death."

"That's pretty serious thinking. Does she have any proof?"

"No. And I can't believe that Rebecca would do something like that."

"You don't know anything about her. Where she came from. What she's doing here by herself. Do you think you should try to find out something about her past?"

"I'd feel like a snoop. Wouldn't she tell me if there was anything she wanted me to know?"

Mrs. Thomas frowned for the first time during their conversation. "I guess she would. To tell the truth, I'm most puzzled by her coming here and living up there in that old house by herself. That doesn't seem like something a young woman would do."

The phone interrupted their talk. Mrs. Thomas answered and handed it to Jeffrey. "It's Miranda."

"Jeffrey, survive the storm?" Miranda didn't wait for him to say he did or didn't. "Listen, have lunch with me and Paul. I have some interesting things to report."

"About what?" Jeffrey figured he could guess.

"About your friend on the mountain. Things you need to hear, so say yes or I'm coming over there right now."

"I'll have lunch with you. Sharkey's?"

"If it didn't blow away. I'll call and make sure. Noon if you don't hear from me again."

"Okay." Jeffrey didn't feel good about the money he'd earned working for Rebecca the day before. He'd spend it all taking Miranda and Paul to lunch.

Miranda made it sound as if Jeffrey would be surprised by what she had found out. Maybe he wasn't going to have to snoop, like his mother suggested. Maybe Miranda had done it for him, but he was nervous.

Why are you expecting something bad, Jeff, old man? he questioned himself as he gathered his dishes and sent his mother out of the kitchen.

He realized that he was at the point where nothing he found out about Rebecca would surprise him.

Chapter 13

Miranda and Paul were waiting for him at a table in Sharkey's. Jeffrey was glad to see them. Gathering here reminded him of when life was normal — whatever normal was. He would have to work hard not to expect Barbara to come in, her long red hair bouncing around her shoulders, an apologetic manner for being the last one to arrive. Then he remembered that Barbara had gotten her beautiful hair cut, and the weird way she started dressing before — before —

No more thinking, Jeffrey, he told himself, but he had one more memory.

You would have picked her up. You always picked her up. Yes, yes, I would have.

Jeffrey stopped to talk to Lizzie so his mind would stop playing tricks on him. "Give the check to me, Lizzie. Don't even let Miranda and Paul see it. Today I'm treating and I don't want an argument."

Lizzie grinned and nodded. She lit up at Jeffrey's singling her out to speak to, even about her job. Jeffrey saw how badly she needed to be identified in terms of someone other than Dizzie Lizzie. On impulse, he leaned over and kissed her on the cheek. He was feeling really needy himself lately.

"What are you doing, Thomas?" Paul said, giving Jeffrey a high five. "Guaranteeing good service?" Miranda's rugged, good-looking friend grinned, then reached back over to Miranda and took her hand. None of what Jeffrey was going through — well, not Barbara's death, but the confusion over caring for Rebecca — would have fazed Paul. He had dated a lot before he met Miranda. Jeffrey had gotten involved with Barbara before he had a lot of experience dating. Now he needed experience badly.

"Won't hurt. But I had business to discuss with Lizzie." He let Miranda and Paul wonder what, pulled out a chair, and grabbed a menu from behind the containers of sugar and catsup. "Have you ordered?"

"Waiting for you." Miranda smiled at Jeffrey. "Being here together makes me miss Barbara. I know you do, too, Jeff." Miranda reached over and squeezed Jeffrey's arm.

"Yeah, I was thinking about that when I came in." Jeffrey buried his nose in the menu and studied it. He always ordered the same thing, but he felt like hiding for a minute.

Lizzie hovered at their table, so they told her what they wanted right away. "And bring me a Coke now, please," Jeffrey added.

"Now I know to flirt with the waitress." Paul watched Lizzie hurry back to the counter.

Miranda bounced the menu off his head. "Try it."

They laughed, then fell into an awkward silence. Finally Jeffrey spoke. "So, what did you find out about Rebecca?"

"Nothing." Miranda's voice was flat. "Absolutely nothing."

"You got me out here to tell me *that*?" Jeffrey smiled at Lizzie and sipped the huge Coke she set in front of him.

"That's significant." Miranda leaned forward and spoke in a low voice. "There's no record of anyone buying that old house. There's no record of her buying that red convertible. There's nothing at the motor vehicle bureau. They never heard of vanity plates saying BEKKA. No record of anyone having that plate in this county. There's no sales tax record of her buying the car."

"She may have paid cash at a dealer who doesn't keep good records." Jeffrey thought about what Miranda was saying, trying to find a reason for every detail. "She doesn't pay tax; he doesn't pay tax on the sale."

"The car will be missing from his inventory if anyone ever checks." Paul entered the conversation.

"No one will check. And maybe the dealer never put the car into his inventory. He paid cash for it in the first place."

"There's no record of her birth in this state," Miranda continued.

"She's never said where she's from. Maybe she's from New York or California. Or anywhere. Have you checked birth records all over the United States?"

"Of course not. I'll overlook the birth records. Jeffrey, she's left no paper trail at all." Miranda played with her silverware, knowing she didn't have much evidence, and that Jeffrey wasn't buying into what she did have.

"In a court of law, you have nothing that will stand up as evidence for anything." Jeffrey shook his head. "Are you trying to prove she doesn't exist?" He laughed, but without humor.

"Very funny." Miranda stared across the restaurant. "I just think that coming here all alone, living in that old house, having no real reason to be here — all that sounds strange to me."

"But not illegal. Case closed," Jeffrey said. "When I get to be a super-power lawyer, Miranda, don't apply for a detective's job."

"I wouldn't have tried it now if you weren't such a dweeb, Jeffrey Thomas." Miranda tried a different route. "You're letting yourself be totally hypnotized by Rebecca Webster, and I think you're going to get hurt."

"If he wants to get hurt, Miranda," Paul said, squeezing her arm, "it's his problem. You can't stop him or protect him."

"Well, don't say I didn't tell you so." Miranda reached for her plate from Lizzie, set it down hard, and started eating her hamburger.

"Speak of the devil," Miranda said quietly, "and I was if you weren't, here she comes."

Jeffrey turned around to see Rebecca gliding across the restaurant toward their table. Part of him was glad to see that she was all right after the storm, but part of him didn't want to see her at all right now. He stood up.

"Rebecca, come join us." Jeffrey knew Rebecca didn't need the invitation, but he wanted her to feel comfortable. He hoped Miranda would behave.

"Your mother said you were here." Rebecca's smile made her luminous. She wore a black T-shirt and black tights, leaving no doubt that she had the best figure in town. Her long hair gleamed blue-black like a crow's wing. She tossed it away from her face, slid in past Jeffrey, and took his arm when he sat back down. Her long red fingernails made a vivid contrast with his tanned, muscled arm.

For a few seconds she stared at him as if they were alone, her eyes, her smile inviting him to kiss her, to love her, saying she would welcome his love. He felt sweat on his forehead. He grabbed his Coke and took a big swallow to hide his feelings.

"Have you had lunch? I'll call Lizzie." He would have gotten up and headed for the counter to give himself a minute break, but Rebecca locked her hands around his arm.

"I ate an hour ago. Got up early. If Lizzie comes close, I'll have an iced coffee, but nothing else. Go ahead and eat, all of you." Her eyes met Miranda's. Jeffrey wouldn't have been surprised to see fiery sparks flying all over the table. There was no love lost between these two women.

Rebecca moved even closer to him, keeping her hands on his arm. "Have you been talking about the storm?" Rebecca asked. "Wasn't it wonderful?" Her eyes glittered.

"If you like storms," Miranda said, taking a big breath. "It did a lot of damage in town."

"Did you lose a lot of trees?" Paul asked Rebecca. "On the mountain? It seemed even worse over there."

"A few." Rebecca shrugged. "The sea was fierce. I loved watching it."

"You sat outside watching the ocean?" Jeffrey looked at Rebecca and tried to lift his burger with one hand. The onion and tomato slid out, but he managed to get a bite. It stuck in his throat, though, and tasted like sawdust.

"No." Her dark eyes teased him. "I can see the ocean from the second floor. From my bedroom." Her voice made the word bedroom sound like an invitation. "I have a lovely view."

"When is your family coming, Rebecca?" Miranda asked. "Didn't you say they'd be right behind you, to renovate that old house? It may not be safe for you to live out there alone. Where are your parents from? I don't think you ever said." Suddenly Miranda was extremely friendly.

"No, I didn't, did I? They've been delayed, but I expect them soon. And I'm not a bit afraid out there. Jeffrey and Tony spent the day with me yesterday, and they're planning on coming back a lot. Aren't you, Jeff?"

You wanted to be a lawyer, didn't you, Jef-

frey? Well, here's some practice. Defuse this situation.

"Sure, if you have work to do. It doesn't look as if Mr. Smeal is going back to work at all this summer. Have you found anything else, Paul? Maybe Rebecca has enough work for two."

"Too late in the summer. All the jobs are gone. I don't know if I can get into school or not. I may have to stay out and work for a year. Go up to Boston and get something that pays enough to get some savings."

"You can't do that, Paul." Miranda looked disturbed. "We were going to be freshmen together."

"I've got no choice."

"The summer isn't going as you planned, is it?" The hint of a smile on Rebecca's face said she didn't really care.

"Everything changed when you came to town." Miranda was blunt. "You don't worry about money, Rebecca. That's a great car you're driving. Classic. Did your father buy it for your graduation?"

"No, I bought it myself. I always wanted a convertible. It gives me such a sense of freedom. Let's go for a ride now. I just love driving it." Rebecca stood up and pushed Jeffrey to his feet.

"I have to get back to work," Miranda said. "I do have a summer job. And Paul is driving me, so he has to leave, too."

Lizzie hurried over and handed Jeffrey the bill for lunch. Quickly he stuck it in his pocket. "Lunch is on me, guys. I'll see you later." He looked at Miranda and Paul and tried to smile. Miranda shrugged.

Paul gave Jeffrey a "sorry to leave you alone with that gorgeous woman" look. He grinned.

"Then you can go with me, Jeffrey," Rebecca said, looking up at him. "That's better anyway. I'd much rather have you to myself."

Jeffrey was trapped. She knew he didn't have a summer job. He had nothing to hurry back to at home, no excuse not to spend time with her.

Suddenly he was afraid to be left alone with Rebecca Webster.

Chapter 14

Rebecca drove along the coast without speaking. She sensed that Jeffrey was feeling awkward, and she wanted him to relax. Now that she had control — at last — of her emotions, she wanted to take complete charge of Jeffrey. She knew she had sent him home a couple of times confused and, for all she knew, angry. Except that Jeffrey wasn't the type to get angry often. Hurt, maybe, but he wasn't full of anger. But then, *he* had no reason to be.

She tried not to drive too fast, tried to lean back and relax, let the wind blow through her hair, look beautiful. Twice she glanced over to smile at Jeffrey. He smiled, but immediately looked away. It was time to talk.

When she came to a particularly beautiful overlook, she stopped the car. "I love this view, don't you?"

"Sure," Jeffrey said. "Hard to believe there

was such a storm last night, isn't it? The sea is as smooth as glass."

"Maybe the storm didn't come this far north." Small talk. She wasn't good at it. She drummed her fingers on the steering wheel.

"Jeffrey, I have no idea how much I've confused you or maybe made you angry."

"I don't think I could ever be angry with you, Rebecca."

"Yes, you could." She turned to him and took one hand, reached for the other. "Look at me." She pulled him around so he faced her. "I want you to love me. I *need* you to love me. I — I think that scared me at first. But now I feel good about it."

She couldn't get Jeffrey to look at her. He stared at his lap, then out through the windshield, toward the ocean.

"I don't know, Rebecca. I think — well, this is happening too fast. Too soon after Barbara's death. I really loved Barbara. I'm sure you know that. I'm sure you can understand. We had been together for a long time. And — "

"That doesn't mean you can't love me, Jeffrey. Or that you've stopped loving Barbara. But Barbara is no longer here. And I am. I don't mind if you don't love me as much as you did Barbara. At first. I just need to know that you *could* love me."

She was playing with words, trying to decide what he wanted to hear.

"Come on. Let's get out of the car, sit on those rocks, Jeffrey. I want to feel the breeze off the ocean on my face. I wish we could go to the lake, go out on the boat again, but — well, I guess that would hold bad memories for you." Rebecca scrambled out of the car and ran to sit on some huge rocks on the cliff.

Jeffrey followed slowly. When he came close to her, she pulled him down beside her. "Put your arm around me, Jeffrey. Just sit here and hold me. You aren't afraid of me, are you?"

"Why would I be afraid of you?" Jeffrey said. "That's silly."

"I don't know. I can sense that you're nervous." She snuggled close to him and gave him some time.

Rebecca was too smart, too sensitive to his mood. She realized that he was reluctant to relax and let things go back to the way they were. He was trying, though. He sat on the big rock and tried to enjoy Rebecca leaning into him, her body warm, her hair smelling of fresh air and the perfume that she liked. The scent filled his nostrils and teased his senses.

She was *so* different from Barbara. Her moods flew up and down like the cormorants out there diving for fish. The birds soared up and up, then circled. Suddenly they'd spot lunch and dive, dive deep, then surface holding the fish in their beaks. Rebecca not only soared up and down easily, she sent his emotions up and down like a broken thermometer.

It would be so easy to relax right now and follow her lead, to be completely in love with her. Miranda thought he was going to get hurt. Should he worry about that?

Rebecca turned, tipped her head, offered her lips. Not even hesitating, he leaned down and covered her lips with his. Her mouth was warm, inviting. He kissed her deeply, letting his emotions dive deep, not caring about the consequences. Drowning in the deep water that loving her offered.

Finally she pulled away and gasped. "Oh, Jeffrey, you *do* love me. I have to trust you. You would never hurt me. How could I be afraid of loving you?"

"You've been hurt, haven't you, Rebecca?" Jeffrey stared into her violet eyes, thinking of sun sparkling on the deep sea.

Her eyes changed, darkened. "I was betrayed, Jeffrey. I can never forgive — " She closed her eyes and turned away.

"I would never betray you, Rebecca. But what you're saying makes me know that we have to be careful, go slow. Otherwise we'll risk destroying something that could be special. I want our love to be special." Jeffrey stood up so he wouldn't be tempted to hold Rebecca in his arms again.

He kept talking, pacing back and forth. "I think we should see less of each other. We should let our feelings cool off a little. If what we're feeling is real, it won't go away."

"You don't want to see me again?"

"I didn't say that. Just that we shouldn't see each other as much. I think I need time to sort through how I feel. We might even see other people. There's no one else I want to go out with, but — "

"You can't break up with me now, Jeffrey." She stood and gripped his arm, turning him so he had to look at her.

What he saw in her eyes frightened him again. There was determination, desperation, and anger all mixed together, a lethal mix for settling their problems without an argument. "I didn't say break up, Rebecca. I said cool off."

"But you *meant* break up. You see less and less of me and then you don't see me at all. I know break up when I hear it." Her voice rose higher and higher, filled with anger. She seemed to have one of their terrible summer storms inside of her, ready to crash and ignite the skies with fury.

"Rebecca, I — " He reached for her. She backed away.

"I don't want to stop seeing you, Jeffrey. I don't want to see less of you, either. I want to see *more* of you. I want to be with you every day. Don't tell me you need time. What for? Don't pull away from me now, Jeffrey. I won't let you!"

Chapter 15

She had done it again — gotten angry. She had let her emotions run wild and risked losing everything she had accomplished so far. When she demanded that Jeffrey keep seeing her, he spun around and headed for the car. Sliding into the passenger seat, he slammed the door.

She stared at him, but he wouldn't look at her. Finally she had to get into the car herself. With total disregard for safety she backed up, screeched the brakes, then swung onto the highway. Accelerating swiftly, she let the car climb to fifty, sixty, sixty-five, squealing around the curves, gripping the steering wheel with iron strength, willing the car to stay on the road. Hardly looking ahead, she passed two cars in a no-passing zone. The second car honked at her as she cut back in recklessly to keep from smashing head-on into an approaching truck.

If her driving frightened Jeffrey, and she was sure it did, he said nothing. A stony silence built and built while she sped down the mountain.

Skidding around the turnoff and into Sharkey's parking lot, the car sent gravel flying into other parked cars and the stone post that held the restaurant's sign.

Stomping the brake to the floor, she stopped the bright red convertible, practically standing the car on its nose.

Jeffrey unlatched his door, stepped out, slammed it behind him. She watched him walk to his car, his shoulders squared, his mouth pulled into a severe line.

She pounded the steering wheel with both fists, gritted her teeth together, and watched him pull out and onto the highway without looking at her again.

She had thought this man would be so easily twisted around her fingers, but he was proving to be more stubborn than she'd counted on.

What could she do now?

If she hadn't been so weak — so out of control of her own feelings.

Her rage, her need for revenge grew stronger every second.

She glanced at her watch. The police station

would still be open. Jeffrey would regret pushing her away.

She parked a block away and rehearsed her speech while she walked to the station. A young man with dark, curly hair was at the front desk.

"May I help you?" He stared at Rebecca and she took advantage of his being attracted to her.

"I — well, I hardly know where to start." She smiled at the police officer sweetly. "I'm just so nervous about what I have to do." She twisted her fingers in and out of her car keys, putting on a great show of nerves.

"I'll be glad to help you." He stood up. "But you'll have to tell me what this is about."

"I need to talk to Detective Radler. He helped us when Barbara Matthew was drowned in that awful boat accident on the lake."

"His office is down that hall on the right. Third door. Maybe I'd better show you."

The police officer came out from behind the desk and stood looking down at Rebecca.

"You're very tall. I like tall men."

She took his arm which was certainly not what he expected her to do. His face turned bright pink, and he started walking to hide his embarrassment. He stopped at Detective Radler's office and pointed her inside.

"Thank you so much, Officer Callihan." She read his name tag. "You have been very kind."

"You're welcome. Anytime." He ducked his head and practically ran back to his desk.

Rebecca smiled. She let her smile for the young police officer include Detective Radler as she turned to him.

"Miss Webster." Detective Radler stood. "Am I right? You were at the party with Barbara Matthew who went on that boat and was drowned."

"Yes, I was. You have a wonderful memory. That was a terrible accident, but I'm afraid I have a confession to make. This is so hard for me, and I know I didn't do the right thing at the time. My conscience has bothered me ever since."

"You have something to add to your story?" Radler pointed to a chair indicating that Rebecca should sit.

She perched on the edge of the chair and leaned forward, clutching the edge of the desk firmly. "I just felt so sorry for Jeffrey Thomas I didn't say anything at the time. And I didn't think it was important. But the more I thought about it, the more I thought maybe it *was* important."

"Go on, Miss Webster." Detective Radler

wasn't as taken with her as the young man at the front desk, so Rebecca looked totally serious and started her story.

"Well, while we were on the boat, just a short time before that storm came up and Barbara disappeared, I overheard a fight between Barbara and Jeffrey."

"And you thought that wasn't important to tell us at the time?" Radler thumped a pencil on his notebook.

"I knew it was important, but I didn't want to get Jeffrey in trouble."

"And now you do?"

"Oh, no. And I'm sure this still isn't very important, but I couldn't keep it secret any longer. I was so upset at the time. . . . Anyway, during the fight, Jeffrey told Barbara he was going to break up with her. I think you know they had been going together for a long time."

"Yes, we knew that."

"I didn't know *why* Jeffrey was breaking off their relationship, but Barbara got really angry. That was, after she begged and pleaded with him *not* to break up. When he insisted, she got mad and told him he couldn't do that, she wouldn't let him. 'You won't let me?' Jeffrey said. 'How can you stop me?' 'I have my ways,' Barbara said. And Jeffrey said, 'So do I, Barbara. You can't hold onto me against my will.' "

"What did Mr. Thomas do then?"

"He ran away from the party toward the boat dock, leaving Barbara behind. I heard Barbara crying, and then I stopped listening."

"I thought you said you heard the argument on the boat?"

"Oh, did you think I said that? I wasn't on the boat, remember. I heard them fighting at the party."

"So you think Jeffrey killed Barbara when she refused to break off with him?"

"Oh, I didn't say that, either, Detective Radler. I have no idea if her death was an accident or not, but I do know Jeffrey was really angry when he left the party."

Radler made some notes, then looked back at Rebecca. "Is there anything else you want to add to your story?"

"No, I think I've told you everything now. I'm sorry I didn't tell you earlier, but no one asked me anything and at the time I — I — well, like I say, I didn't want Jeffrey to get in trouble. Unless he — unless — "

"Unless he killed Barbara Matthew."

Rebecca stared at her fingers, clutching the

desk, and relaxed them, moving them into her lap. "Yes," she whispered.

"What do *you* think, Miss Webster?" Radler stood up, indicating their meeting was over.

"About Jeffrey? Whether or not he would do that? I don't know, sir. I'm new in town, and I don't really know Jeffrey Thomas that well. I was just getting to know all those people. Barbara was such a sweet person. I can't believe she's gone."

She didn't like the way Detective Radler looked at her. As if he wondered why she had come in here now, why she had waited to tell her story. Or maybe, as if he didn't think she was telling the truth. He certainly couldn't prove it one way or the other. Surely he'd follow up on what she'd told him.

"Thank you for coming in, Miss Webster. We'll check into what you say you heard."

Rebecca turned and tried to control her temper until she got outside the police station. Detective Radler was suspicious of her. She knew it.

But it wouldn't do any good to get angry with him. She breathed deeply a few times and headed back to her car. She didn't care one way or another about what Detective Radler thought about her story. He'd *have* to follow it up.

She had done all she could think of right now to make Jeffrey's life miserable. He would know Rebecca Webster would not be betrayed a second time.

Chapter 16

Jeffrey hadn't been home long when his mother called him. He had been sitting, staring out the window, trying to calm down, to get over the frightening ride down the mountain.

"Jeffrey, some people want to see you down here," his mother said from the bottom of the stairs.

"It's the police," Tony called out. "Wonder what they want?"

"Keep wondering, Tony, while you go outside and play." Mrs. Thomas took a firm hold on Tony's arm and led him back toward the kitchen. "Want me to help you, Jeffrey?"

"No, that's okay, Mom." Jeffrey wanted to say, Yes, please stay, please don't leave me alone, but he was eighteen years old. He knew the police officers were there about the boat accident. Maybe they had more questions. Maybe they'd found out something new.

"Mr. Thomas, maybe you remember that I'm Detective Radler." The man dressed in a brown suit stretched his hand toward Jeffrey.

Jeffrey took it in a firm grasp. "Certainly, I remember you, sir." How could I forget, he thought. You made me tell that awful story over a million times.

"We have a few more questions we'd like to ask you, if you don't mind." The officer pointed Jeffrey to a chair in the living room. Then he perched on the edge of the sofa beside a uniformed policeman who had made himself comfortable.

"I don't mind if you think it will help." Jeffrey minded a lot, but he couldn't say so. He couldn't scream at the man to leave him alone, stop reminding him of that terrible day. Stop putting the picture of Barbara in her coffin back into his head. What else was there to add to the story?

"We've had some new evidence come to light." Detective Radler started talking. "And it concerns you."

Jeffrey nodded. His stomach churned and twisted into knots. He didn't like the way Radler looked at him. As if on one hand he felt sorry for Jeffrey, but on the other he was pleased to confront him again.

"A witness has come forth and said that you

and your friend Barbara Matthew had a fight just before the storm came up. That you — well, that you may have threatened her. Is that true?"

"Who is your witness, Detective Radler?" Jeffrey's case of nerves vanished. Replacing it was a fiery anger that honed his voice to a steel edge.

"That doesn't matter, son. Just answer my questions. Did you and Miss Matthew have a fight just before she drowned?"

"*We did not.* Your witness is lying."

"It's in your interest to say that," the police officer stated quietly. He had taken out a pencil and paper to write Jeffrey's statement.

"I told you this before. Barbara and I had a discussion at the party. She asked me to come away and talk to her — alone — so we went out on the boat. We thought we were alone on the boat." Jeffrey's debating skills, the same skills he would use as a lawyer if he ever got through law school, came to his aid. "Detective Radler, remember that I said Rebecca Webster showed up on the boat with us. She denied it, and a few people testified they saw her at the party after we'd left. Could those people have been mistaken about the time they saw Rebecca?"

Jeffrey stopped to take a breath. He studied

Radler, who was giving Jeffrey his full attention. He'd give the man that.

"If Rebecca Webster is your witness, doesn't that prove I wasn't lying? She would have had to have been on the boat to have heard this alleged argument." Jeffrey was working in the dark. He and Barbara had scarcely talked at all. She'd said she felt sick almost immediately and had gone below.

"Can you think of a reason Miss Webster would lie, Jeffrey? About being on the boat or hearing this conversation?"

"I can. Rebecca and I had a fight this afternoon. She gets a little weird when she's angry."

"You have a lot of trouble with women, don't you, Thomas?" The police officer who'd come with Radler spoke at last.

Jeffrey shot him a nasty glance. But the remark didn't matter, and Jeffrey couldn't let it distract his thinking. "If Miss Webster came to you with this story today, I think she may have been angry enough to want to cause trouble for me."

"Are you saying she's lying?" Radler got up and paced the floor.

"Depends on who you want to believe. I don't deny I was considering breaking up with Barbara Matthew, but I had not told Barbara.

I never once mentioned it. I hadn't decided."

"Between the two women." The police officer seemed determined to make Jeffrey angry — or guilty.

Again, Jeffrey tried to ignore him. He stared at Detective Radler, letting him make the next move.

"Jeffrey, Miranda Stevens told me in the initial investigation that she suspected Miss Webster of killing Barbara Matthew. Do you have an opinon about that?"

"How could Rebecca kill Barbara if she wasn't on the boat? How could she have overheard this fight if she wasn't on the boat? We didn't have any discussion about our relationship at the party. Barbara wanted to talk about something else that had just happened to her. I never found out what that was."

The corner of Radler's mouth lifted slightly, as if he wanted to smile but felt it inappropriate behavior. "Perhaps I need to speak to Miss Webster again. There do seem to be some discrepancies in her story, but I wanted to talk to you again, Jeffrey. Off the record, totally off the record" — Radler glanced at the officer — "would you say that Rebecca Webster is capable of killing anyone?"

The question seemed unfair, whether on or off the record. How could Jeffrey know that answer? He thought it over, though, recalled Rebecca's face when she was angry, the fire in her eyes, her strange moods. He thought about the times he'd felt almost afraid when he was with her, when he realized not seeing her again would be a relief.

"I — I — " he stammered and hated himself for doing so. "I don't think I can answer that question."

"You can't or you won't?" Radler insisted.

"I can't." If Jeffrey knew, he would give an opinion. The idea was too impossible to imagine.

He was surprised, however, to feel a chill travel the length of his body, to feel his heart ice over. Did he know the answer and not want to admit it?

"Thank you, Jeffrey." Detective Radler reached for Jeffrey's hand again.

Reluctantly Jeffrey grasped the man's hand, hoping Radler wouldn't notice — wouldn't ask him why he was so cold.

He watched the two get in their car and leave. Then he continued to stare out the picture window of his house, not seeing anything.

All of a sudden he was back on the boat, trying to keep it afloat in the wind that rocked it from side to side, the waves that crashed against the sides and threatened to swamp the small craft. The cold wind roared in his ears, whipped around his body, stiffening his arms, his legs. He saw himself go down onto his knees, felt the water swirl around him.

But this time, just before he blacked out, he heard the scream. He heard Barbara scream out and call his name. "Jeffrey! Jeffrey! Please, please, help me. Jeffrey, help me."

Silence. Pure, simple silence. And the terrible cold.

Finally he came back to his own living room where he shivered, still staring outside. He shook his head, turned, and headed for the kitchen to get something hot to drink.

Had he really heard Barbara scream that day, or was his mind playing tricks on him? All he remembered at the time was fighting to stay afloat, a dream about Rebecca, then blackness.

The teakettle shrieked at him. He grabbed it, unable to stand the sound.

"Jeffrey, there you are. What did the police want? I saw them leave, but I was outside." Before Jeffrey could tell his mother what the police had said, she cut him off with another question. "Has Tony been in here? I sent him outside to play, but I told him not to go out of the yard."

"No, I haven't seen Tony." Jeffrey searched

the cupboard for a tea bag. The box he reached for was empty.

"Did Rebecca find you? What did she want?"

"Rebecca? Rebecca was here?" He gripped the teakettle, his knuckles turning white as the metal bit into the palm of his hand.

"She pulled up just after the police left. She said she wanted to take you and Tony to dinner. I told her you were in the living room, and that I was looking for Tony. She said she'd help me search and talk to you later."

"Mother — " Jeffrey caught his breath and leaned on the counter as a stab of fear cut across his chest.

"Do you think Tony would have gone off alone with her?" his mother asked. "Surely not, since she was looking for the two of you."

Without another word, Jeffrey grabbed his mother's car keys from the hook on the kitchen bulletin board and dashed out the door.

Rebecca was angry. She had gone to the police and lied. Now had she coaxed Tony into her car?

Do you think Miss Websler is capable of killing anyone, Jeffrey? Detective Radler's words echoed in Jeffrey's mind.

What is Rebecca Webster capable of when she's angry, Jeffrey? Do you know? Can you imagine?

He couldn't imagine. No, he didn't want to imagine what Rebecca might do because she was angry with him.

All he knew was that an unreasonable fear filled him, pumped adrenaline throughout his body, and sent him roaring down the street, out toward the highway, up the mountain to find Tony. To find his brother and Rebecca Webster before anything he could imagine came true.

Chapter 17

Miranda looked up as she and Paul got out of Paul's car and started into Sharkey's. She was just in time to see Jeffrey speed by on the highway.

"Wasn't that Jeffrey? In his mother's car?"

Paul said, "It sure was. I looked to see who was driving so fast."

"I think there's trouble. Let's follow him."

"How do we know where he's going? He's gone." No matter what Paul was saying, he was getting back into his car at the same time.

"I'm sure there's only one place Jeffrey can be going from here at that speed. And it has to do with Rebecca. Let's go up there. I'd be glad to be wrong." Miranda was buckled up, ready for Paul to drive as fast as Jeffrey was moving.

Paul backed, turned, and spewed gravel as he pulled out of Sharkey's lot and onto the highway. He headed south, then swung around the sharp turn that started up the mountain.

"We're going to feel foolish if Jeffrey is only in a hurry to see Rebecca." Paul glanced at Miranda.

"Let's feel foolish," Miranda said. "But if he's that eager to see her, I'm going to give up discouraging him from dating her."

"I know you're still upset about Barbara, Miranda." Paul's face was serious, his hands in a tight grip on the steering wheel as he negotiated the mountain curves. "But can't you accept the idea that Jeffrey might really care for Rebecca?"

"No, I can't. I know her. She delights in winning Jeffrey over, but if she gets tired of him, she won't hesitate to hurt him. He's been hurt enough."

The summer evenings were long and daylight lasted until nine o'clock in town, but on the tree-lined road, shadows treacherously threw their dark shapes. Miranda knew that Paul was probably blind every time he skidded from light to dark. "Be careful, Paul. Let's get there in one piece."

"You're right." He slowed. "I'm never going to catch up with Jeffrey anyway."

As Paul pulled his Jeep into the driveway at

Rebecca's, Jeffrey's car was there. Jeffrey came running from the house.

"Miranda! Paul!" he shouted. "I don't know what you're doing here, but I'm sure glad to see you. I need help."

Miranda said, "We saw you drive by Sharkey's like a bat out of hell. What's wrong?" Miranda took Jeffrey's arm, hoping to calm him a little.

"I — " Jeffrey had to stop and take a deep breath so he could talk. "I'm sure Rebecca has Tony."

"She has *Tony*?" Miranda's heart leaped and her own breath stilled.

"What makes you think that?" Paul asked the next question, before Miranda could speak again. "And why — "

"It's a long story," Jeffrey interrupted. "Rebecca and I had a fight, and she threatened me. She told the police a story that sent them after me again, but while I was talking to them, she came to the house and lured Tony away."

"You think she'd hurt Tony just because she's mad at *you*?" Miranda regained her voice.

"I don't know what she's capable of, Miranda, but I'm starting to think you might be right."

"Right?"

"At first she told the police she heard Barbara and me fighting on the boat. That placed her there, after she said she was only at the party. If she *was* on the boat . . ."

Miranda still didn't have any proof, but her gut instinct told her Rebecca was capable of murder. But why? "Surely she won't hurt Tony, Jeffrey. She only wanted you here."

"I'd like to think that, but I have to find him. Help me look for them. They aren't in the house." Jeffrey took off, running down the path toward the ocean.

He fought back total panic and scrambled down the steep path. Several times he skidded on the loose dirt and stones, but he regained his balance and continued at breakneck speed. All he needed was to see Tony.

He didn't know if Rebecca would bring Tony out here just to get him to follow her. But if that was so, she'd gotten her way. He'd listen to whatever she needed to say to him. But please, please, let Tony be safe.

The sun was low on the western horizon. This was a perfect time to be here — cool, quiet, except for a few gulls circling and calling to each other.

Once on the beach, Jeffrey shaded his eyes and looked in both directions. The tide was coming in fast, lapping at the dry sand. Hardly able to see because of the glare, he walked quickly toward where Rebecca and Tony had done their tide pooling the last time they were here.

Huge black rocks stuck up out of the water like the heads of seals, smoothed by time and erosion. Waves sloshed over and around them, leaving lacy foam on the beach, spewing into the sky farther out where rocks were nearly covered.

Miranda caught up with Jeffrey. "I don't see anyone. Let's yell. Tony. *Toe-neee.*" She drew out the syllables. Her voice echoed across the rocks and blended with the rush of water in and out.

"*To-ny,*" Jeffrey yelled even louder.

Was he upset for no reason? Maybe Rebecca hadn't even brought Tony here. Maybe by now Tony was home in the kitchen, eating a good dinner while Jeffrey was out here yelling and calling out to the wind and the gulls.

Tony had probably gone down the street to get his friend Brian to come and see the police car.

But Jeffrey wanted to make sure.

"*To-ny,*" he yelled again. Then he listened.

"Did you hear something?" Paul said. "I thought I heard a voice."

Jeffrey ran toward the spit of land that reached out into the sea, but now was almost covered with water. Grabbing roots that an even higher tide had exposed, he swung around and over the sandy bank that rose to meet the cliffs.

"Toe-neee." Miranda followed, calling over and over.

"Jeff!" A thin cry reached their ears. Fog was gathering farther out, swirling and heading to shore. Thin wisps circled the taller rocks on this side of the spit. "Jeff, help me!"

"There!" Miranda pointed. "He's way out there on that rock. Oh, Jeffrey, it's nearly underwater. Can Tony swim?"

"In a pool." Jeffrey jerked off his jean jacket, shirt, and shoes. Unbuckling his belt, he let his jeans slide to his bare feet. "But no one could swim in this rising tide, with all these rocks to get thrown against." He kicked the jeans aside.

"Can you get out there in time?"

"I have to, Miranda!" Jeffrey waded into the water only to be hit by a bigger than usual wave that knocked him off his feet.

Even he couldn't fight this monster surf.

Chapter 18

Paul waded into the water alongside Jeffrey.
Every time the tide rushed in, the two boys
grabbed each other to keep their footing. If
one of them tumbled down, they would be
quickly bashed against the rocky ocean floor.
When the ocean whooshed out, water pulled
at them, sand slid out from under their feet,
threatening to drag them along to deeper
water.

"I've never seen the surf this high except
in a storm. Tony could never stand up here,"
Jeffrey said, shouting to be heard above the
crashing waves. "I'm having a hard time staying on my feet." Jeffrey slipped and barely kept
from being caught in the undertow of the next
wave.

"He did the right thing to climb up on those
rocks." Paul wiped salty spray from his face.

"Except that those rocks will be underwater

in a few minutes." Jeffrey fought to hurry. "Hang on, Tony," he yelled as they worked their way closer and closer. "We're coming."

The sunset caught and painted Tony's already pale face silver, making him seem even more terrified.

He practically jumped from the top of the rock when Jeffrey reached him. He wrapped his arms around Jeffrey's neck in a death grip. "I knew you'd come, Jeff. I knew it. I kept thinking about you and saying, Come, come on, Jeff. I was so scared."

Tony shivered with cold and fear. He was choking Jeffrey, but his skinny arms tightly clinging to Jeffrey's neck felt wonderful.

"I know, Tony, I know. I must have heard you right off, since I broke all the speed limits getting here. You should have seen me." Jeffrey hugged Tony even tighter. "But what are you doing out here anyway?" Jeffrey figured he knew, but he wanted to hear Tony's story.

While Tony talked in a high, thin voice, shaky with leftover panic, Jeffrey waded back to the beach. With a rhythmic smash against their backs and shoulders, incoming waves roared and tumbled in, soaking them in icy water. Receding waves ripped the sand from beneath their bare feet, pulled and tugged the three of them back out to deep water. Paul gripped Jeffrey's arm, helping him stay up-right. Jeffrey resolved never to tease Paul about his first-string linesman's physique again. Paul's strength gave Jeffrey the confidence he needed to get out of the boiling surf.

"Rebecca said we were going to have a cookout on the beach. She said you would come as soon as you talked to the police, but she wanted me to ride with her and look for wood to build a bonfire." Tony's story was accompanied by chattering teeth, and when he stopped talking, he stammered getting started again.

"You were looking for firewood in the tide pools?" Jeffrey looked at Paul. Paul's serious face reflected how Jeffrey felt. They both realized how close they'd come to losing Tony.

Was Rebecca that naive? Didn't she realize how treacherous the undertow could be with the tide coming in? Jeffrey couldn't believe she'd put Tony's life in danger.

"S-sometimes d-driftwood is in the r-rocks," Tony stuttered. Jeffrey could feel his small body shaking. They needed some blankets, and a fire would feel wonderful.

The fog was getting thicker, starting to swirl and gather in a slight breeze that teased their wet bodies. As the fog rolled in, the waves seemed to get higher and louder. Surely there was a storm far out at sea. This coast didn't get a surf this high and dangerous.

At the beach, the last wave that caught them knocked Jeffrey to his knees, tumbling Tony into Miranda's arms. Tony tried to laugh, but his giggle turned into a whimper, then full-blown crying. Once he started, he couldn't stop.

"It's all right," Miranda said in a soothing voice. "I've got you now and I'll never let you go. You're all right, Tony. Just wet and cold. Here, we'll let Jeffrey have his jeans, but not his shirt."

Miranda peeled Tony's T-shirt off over his head and wrapped him in Jeffrey's dry shirt. She rocked him back and forth until he got quiet and stopped shaking.

Jeffrey pulled on his jeans, jean jacket, shoes, and socks, but even with the jacket he was still shivering himself. He paced back and forth beside Miranda and Tony, rubbing his arms.

Paul had not stood around shivering. As soon as he had his clothes and tennis shoes back on, he took off running along the beach and up the cliff path. In a short time he returned with a blanket and a beach towel.

"Here, Miranda, wrap Tony in this blanket from the car. That'll speed his recovery." He handed Jeffrey the towel. "I'm warm now from running, but I'll dry my hair when you're finished with it."

Jeffrey took back his T-shirt when Miranda wrapped Tony in the wool blanket. "That feels good. Thanks, Paul." Tony looked up and grinned.

"You're welcome, buddy."

"Did you see Rebecca up there? I have to talk to her," Jeffrey said.

"No, I didn't see anyone. No sign of life anywhere out here, except for gulls and beached whales." Now Paul gathered Tony, wrapped in the blanket, into his arms. He got ready to carry him to the car.

Paul led the way down the beach. "We can take Tony home, Jeff, if you want to try to find Rebecca and talk to her."

"I don't like the idea of leaving Jeffrey here alone with that girl." Miranda put her arm around Jeffrey and walked beside him. "You're still cold." She wrapped them both in the beach towel.

"I'm not as easily led astray as Tony," Jeffrey said quietly to her. "But you might keep me from strangling her."

Jeffrey spoke without thinking. Treating *him* badly was one thing. Almost getting Tony drowned was another.

"Surely she didn't mean for Tony to get hurt," Paul said, watching his footing in the growing dusk.

Miranda looked at Jeffrey. They knew better, Jeffrey thought. Miranda had suspected that Rebecca was capable of murder ever since Barbara was killed. Jeffrey was beginning to accept that idea.

"I'd still like to think that," Jeffrey said. "She acted as if she was crazy about him."

"Maybe something happened to cause her to leave him alone." Paul lifted Tony to his other shoulder.

"Want me to carry him?" Jeffrey said.

"No, I'm fine."

As they reached the steep path up the cliff to the house, where they'd left their cars, Paul spoke again.

"What if you don't find her? Why don't you wait until tomorrow to talk to her, Jeff? This fog is going to be hard enough to drive home in now. The darker it gets, the more dangerous that mountain road will be."

"I'll find her," Jeffrey said softly. He had the strange sensation of being watched.

"Rebecca's up there." Tony had his face buried in Paul's shoulder. Now he looked up and pointed.

Standing at the top of the path, on the edge

of the cliff, a dark shadowy figure waited. As Tony pointed his finger, the fog swirled, drifted to leave a clearing. Jeffrey could easily see Rebecca's face, looking down on them.

She was dressed in a long, black dress. Around her shoulders a cloak billowed in the breeze. The hood was crumpled on her shoulders, leaving her black hair to float around her face, framing her features in a soft, dark halo. Across that beautiful face flitted a smile, a small, evil smile. A smile that almost froze Jeffrey's blood.

Chapter 19

Jeffrey said, "I'm going to talk to Rebecca." He took off running up the cliff path.

He didn't know what he was going to say to Rebecca beyond, "Why did you bring Tony out here and leave him stranded on the rocks?" But that was a start.

The knot in his stomach changed from fear to anger, growing and twisting, eager to unleash itself on anyone who would try to hurt Tony.

Wind whistled across the top of the cliff. He looked right, left, but saw no one. Where was she? She had been standing at the top of the path when she looked down on them. How could she just fade away into the mist?

"Rebecca, where are you?" His words swirled through the fog and into the distance. Surely she heard him.

"Did you find her?" Miranda and Paul

reached the top of the pathway. Miranda was out of breath as if they'd run.

"No. I think she's playing some sort of game with us."

"Jeff, I'm hungry," Tony said. "Rebecca said we were going to cook out on the beach."

"I think there's been a change of plan." Jeffrey ran his fingers through Tony's hair. "We *could* all go back to town. I can settle this with Rebecca tomorrow."

At that moment the fog cleared enough so that Jeffrey spotted Rebecca, looking out over the ocean again.

"There she is," Miranda whispered. "She acts as if she never saw us, as if we aren't even here."

"I know she saw us." Jeffrey's frustration was growing. "What is she looking at out there?"

Miranda looked at Paul, still holding Tony. "Paul, would you take Tony back to town? He needs to eat, have a hot bath, and get into bed. I'll help Jeffrey catch up with Rebecca and meet you at my place later."

"You don't have to do this, Miranda." Jeffrey watched as fog swirled and Rebecca disappeared again. "This is my business, and I'll take care of it."

Jeffrey turned to his brother. "Tony, did

Rebecca suggest you go way out into the tide pools this afternoon? Was that her idea or yours? Tell me the truth. I'm not going to scold you or tell Mom. This can be our secret."

"We went down there together and Rebecca helped me look for a little while," Tony said. "Then she said she'd start building the fire if I'd keep looking. She said she had seen a lot of wood stuck out there in those rocks."

"Didn't you see the tide coming in?" Jeffrey asked. "We've talked about being careful when we've been out here."

"I could see the tops of a lot of rocks. I walked on them. By the time I got to those big ones, where Rebecca said the wood was stuck, the rocks behind me were gone. I was too scared to come back."

"Did you ask Rebecca to help you?" Miranda asked.

"She said she couldn't swim. For me to stay where I was on the rocks. She'd go for help."

"Where was she going to go?" Miranda looked at Jeffrey. "All the way to town?"

"Go home, Miranda." Jeffrey couldn't stand around talking any longer. "I'm going to search until I find Rebecca."

"I'm not leaving you behind, Miranda," Paul said. "If this girl is dangerous — well, I'm not leaving you. I'll take Tony up to the house and build a fire in one of the fireplaces. He can get warm there. We'll give you a half hour, or forty-five minutes at the most. Bring Rebecca back to the house. We'll all talk to her."

Miranda looked at Jeffrey and shrugged. "Okay, I'll agree to that plan."

Jeffrey hurried off in the direction they had seen Rebecca. The cottony mist closed around him in no time, so he could barely see any distance ahead. It still wasn't dark, but it might as well have been.

"Rebecca." He yelled her name, not knowing how else to find her. He didn't think she was going to come up to him. She was playing her own game of hide-and-seek, and right now she was winning.

He stopped. Listened. He heard no footsteps behind or ahead. "Miranda?" He thought she was right behind him.

Now she didn't answer. If Rebecca was dangerous, she could hurt Miranda, too. He never should have let her stay with him.

"Miranda!" He yelled her name. Suddenly it seemed more imperative to find her than Rebecca.

The laughter reached him from close by, but he couldn't tell which direction. A voice swirled with the fog and came at him from everywhere.

"Mi-ran-da." Rebecca echoed his words. "Miranda, come here."

Jeffrey spun around and ran back the way he'd come. Then he heard Rebecca's laughter farther in the woods, as if she was on her way back to the old house. He turned, headed in that direction, alert for trees and bushes, since he was off the path.

Ahead, in a clearing, he glimpsed the dark dress and cloak that Rebecca was wearing. The same puff of wind that cleared the fog sent her skirts swirling.

"Rebecca, stop. Wait for me. Please." He ran, then stopped in the space where she'd been standing. How could she keep fading in and out of the trees? Why couldn't he catch up to her when she was so close to him?

She was in control here and she knew it. He spun around and around as laughter closed in on all sides.

Chapter 20

Miranda kept hearing Rebecca's laughter and footsteps on the path, but no matter how close she thought she was, she couldn't catch up with her. She heard Jeffrey call out to her, but by the time she reached where she thought he was, he was gone, too. She realized that separating from him was a mistake. She didn't want to be alone.

The frustrating part was that it wasn't totally dark, but the fog was so thick. Trees were shadowy stick figures looming up in front of her, startling her, making her put up a hand to protect herself.

On the other side of a particularly large tree, in a clearing, Rebecca stood in plain sight. Miranda came on her unexpectedly. Both froze as if in a photo shoot. Then Rebecca turned, floated away, or so it seemed, leaving Miranda staring after her.

When she could move, Miranda stepped over to where Rebecca had stared at a gravestone in the old cemetery. What she read on the stone shocked her. *This wasn't possible!*

"Miranda, come." Rebecca's voice floated through the woods begging Miranda to follow. "Come. Come with me."

Without meaning to, Miranda took a few steps in the direction from which Rebecca spoke. The voice called from behind. She spun around. From the right. The left.

Miranda looked down to read the gravestone again, and it was gone, lost in the mist. She ran back. Nothing. Ran again, stopped just short of hitting a tree.

The damp, cottony mist filled her nostrils, choked her, rested heavy on her chest, keeping her from taking a deep breath. Shallow gulps of air didn't satisfy her. She felt as if she'd run a mile. Her heart pounded and her temples throbbed.

Soon she recognized the cliff path under her feet and felt reassured that she wasn't lost. She slowed down, stepped carefully, making sure she didn't drop into the churning surf.

A swirl of breeze cleared the air for a few seconds, and Miranda peered ahead. She caught a glimpse of a figure in a dark cape, her clothing billowing around her, sailing her forward quickly like a small ship on the ocean.

"Rebecca! Please! Stop!" Miranda called.

The fog closed around them again and the figure disappeared. Miranda knew Rebecca could hear her. This was a game of follow the leader.

Miranda felt her anger growing. She fought it back, knowing that if she let emotion take over she would act foolishly. She must keep her wits about her. Think ahead.

With a sudden blast of air, the fog cleared around her again. Miranda stopped abruptly. Ahead, on the path, Rebecca waited, a smile on her face. Her long black hair tumbled around her shoulders with wild abandon. Her violet eyes glittered with what Miranda could identify with only one word. Evil.

Miranda shivered but took a deep breath and held her ground. She'd take an approach that Rebecca wouldn't expect.

"Rebecca, are you all right?"

"Of course I am. Were you worried?"

"We found Tony in trouble. We got him off the rocks just in time. But no one knew where you were. Tony said you went for help, but — "

"This is none of your business, Miranda. Go home. Take Tony. My business is with Jeffrey." Rebecca spoke almost as if she was giving Miranda a chance to escape some danger. Miranda didn't know how to answer her. Business — a strange word to use. What did she mean?

"What does that gravestone mean, Rebecca? What is this 'business' you have with Jeffrey?"

"You could never understand."

"I could try. Tell me." Miranda made her voice coaxing, sympathetic, a voice she would use for an angry, out-of-control child.

Rebecca tipped her head back and laughed. The wind rose, shrieked as if to compete with Rebecca's voice, as if to drown out anyone who dared make another sound.

Whipping the ribbon from around her neck, Rebecca stepped toward Miranda, reaching out for her.

Miranda stepped backward, holding out both hands to defend herself. Rebecca's cloak flapped in the rising wind. The black velvet ribbon curled and twisted in her fingers like something alive, a poisonous snake writhing before it struck.

The hand that gripped Miranda's arm was like a steel band trapping her. Miranda fought, her free hand grasping the cloak, kicking out with one foot to make Rebecca release her.

But Miranda was no match for Rebecca. Her

strength was unreal. With ease she twisted Miranda in her arms, swung the ribbon around her neck, and started to pull it tight. Nothing was going to stop her from getting to Jeffrey.

With both hands, Miranda grabbed at the narrow band of velvet, trying to keep it from crushing her windpipe, closing off her throat. Was this how Rebecca had killed Barbara? Miranda knew it now for sure. But it was too late. What good would knowing be if Miranda was found dead on this path?

A last bit of strength came from desperation. Miranda bent over and kicked backward, trying to make Rebecca lose her balance. She'd have to let go of the ribbon, giving Miranda a breath of air and one more chance to get away.

Her move worked. Miranda was free. Gulping in the damp air, she managed to speak. "I know that you killed Barbara."

Rebecca's face contorted. "And what will you do about it?" She stepped toward Miranda, reaching for her again.

Miranda didn't have time to look around to see where Rebecca was standing. Her only instinct was to escape, to back away. Her foot reached behind her but found only empty space. Before she could regain her balance, she was falling.

She grasped for a rock, but felt it and the dirt that surrounded it crumble in her hand and cascade around her. She grasped a clump of grass only to have it tear loose. Her fingers closed over scraggly, thin tree roots that slid across her palm, cut deep into her flesh, then finally broke.

She searched frantically for anything to stop her fall. She slid down and off the cliff, sailing toward the crashing surf and rocks below, to certain death.

A lone, thin scream blended into the wind's high, shrieking wail.

Chapter 21

Jeffrey heard Miranda's scream. Despite the fact that he could barely see, he took off running toward the sound.

As he neared the cliffs, he heard the wind whistle and shriek, then moan like a woman crying. He heard Rebecca laugh. The sound sent an even deeper fear through his body. If Rebecca had hurt Miranda . . .

Or worse. If Miranda — he couldn't think. There wasn't time. He needed to get there and help Miranda if he could.

Rebecca saw him coming and ran.

"Rebecca, stop! Where's Miranda? Come back. You have to help me." He knew his begging Rebecca for help was useless, but he was yelling without any thought. Hoping against all hope — "Miranda, can you hear me? Miranda, where are you?"

He stood, staring out to sea, the last of the

light fast disappearing. Waves crashed on the rocks below, echoing with their booming power. A crow mocked his words and dived at him. Then the dark bird circled and disappeared.

Jeffrey knelt on the damp path and looked around. From the height of the cliff, he would never be able to see the difference between rocks, tumbled logs, or a body. All the forms below were dark, shadowy shapes, and there were only a few moments of dim light left. Soon he would be able to see nothing. It was a miracle that the fog had dissipated momentarily.

"Miranda!" He called out one more time. Could Miranda have escaped, run back to the house after she screamed? He was about to hope that was the case and give up when he heard a slight whimper, a tiny moaning sound below. "Miranda?" He yelled again and searched the cliff wall for any movement.

"Jeffrey." The word was almost a whisper, but he knew he heard his name.

Many feet below, he saw her. Miranda.

"Are you hurt? Can you climb back up here? I can't reach you." He needed a rope, a pole, something to lower to Miranda. Something for her to grab onto so he could pull her up before she fell all the way to the beach. The ground was too crumbly for him to attempt to climb down. Both of them could be stuck on the cliff or fall to the rocks below if he slipped.

He stood up and slid out of his jean jacket. The sturdy cloth was as good as a rope. Taking hold of one sleeve, he wrapped his hand in the arm and lowered the rest of the jacket, the other sleeve dangling. No good. Not nearly close enough.

He called to Miranda, "Is there anything to grab onto, to pull yourself up farther?"

Miranda struggled to inch upward. Jeffrey rolled over and slid out of his jeans. He tied the end of one pant leg onto one arm of the jacket. He rebuckled his belt. Twisting his hand into the belt and top of the waist, he lowered the makeshift rope as far as he could reach.

Still not far enough. Miranda would have to climb farther up or inch her way to the bottom. She was much closer to the top, and with high tide, the surf pounded the base of the cliff. It seemed safer to come up the steep embankment.

Time was an enemy. He thought of Paul and Tony at the house. Would Rebecca go back there and try to hurt them?

His stomach tightened, and he started to shiver. The mist and night air chilled his bare legs and seeped into his blood, his bones.

He leaned out and lowered the denim rope again. The jean jacket arm was almost within Miranda's reach.

"Grab hold, Miranda. I can pull you up."

He felt her weight as she wrapped her hand around the sleeve. Praying the knots would hold, he pulled carefully. Hand over hand, he tugged and gathered the strong cotton cloth up under his body for extra security. Rocks bit into his bare legs. His arms ached almost immediately with Miranda's dead weight. Why didn't she help with her legs? She could brace them against the cliff while she hung on.

"Hang on, Miranda," he encouraged her. "I can almost reach you."

When he could grasp her hand and wrist, he felt better. He'd had to trust the jeans to hold, but now he knew he could pull her up. He inched backward, sliding in the dirt, ignoring the dirt and gravel that bit into his bare skin.

Even in the dim light he could see she was in pain. Her face scrunched up, her teeth bit into her bottom lip. With a groan she rolled over the top of the cliff and collapsed with a whimper.

Jeffrey was shaking with cold and tension. He untied his pants from the jacket and slipped into his jeans quickly, brushing caked dirt and tiny rocks from his bare skin.

Miranda was too quiet. He covered her with his jacket and leaned close to her. She appeared to have passed out.

"Miranda? Are you hurt?" He brushed her hair from her face, and she groaned.

Her eyes flew open, eyes filled with fear.

"It's me — Jeffrey. You're all right. You're all right."

"She — I — Rebecca tried — " Miranda sat up and winced in pain. "My leg. I think it's broken." She reached out and felt along her jeans. Then she gasped when she tried to bend her left leg.

"Don't move. Don't try to get up. I'll carry you."

Jeffrey scooped Miranda up and stood, balancing her weight in his arms. She moaned and hugged his chest, crying softly now.

"Oh, Jeffrey, I — Rebecca tried to kill me. First she choked me, then she pushed me off that cliff."

"Don't talk, Miranda. You're all right."

"No, we're not." That was all she said before she passed out. Jeffrey was glad, knowing she had been in pain. He could hurry now, carry her to Paul and they'd get help.

Just before he reached the old house, a crow

sailed down, screeching, diving at them. He ducked his head, wondering why the bird chose to attack them. The bird kept diving at them, cawing. Then it disappeared.

"Miranda!" Paul and Tony sat cross-legged in front of the living room fireplace in the old Branford house. A fire blazed, flames dancing. Seeing them, Paul jumped up and called out. "Is she — is she — "

"She has a broken leg, Paul. Let's get her into your car. You and Tony have to take her to the hospital right away."

They followed Jeffrey outside. Paul opened the back hatch on his Jeep and together they made Miranda as comfortable as possible with a couple of old army blankets.

"Tony," Paul said. "You ride back here with her. I'll drive slowly straight to the hospital, but I don't want her coming to and being alone."

Paul's voice insisted, "Jeffrey, come with us."

"Don't ask me to leave without finding her, Paul. She tried to kill Miranda. I have to believe now that she killed Barbara."

"What will you do if you do find her? She won't come back into town and turn herself over to the police. You know that."

"I don't know what I'll do. I'll decide when I find her."

Paul stared at Jeffrey. Then he headed for the driver's seat of his jeep. "Be careful." He twisted his key in the ignition, started the jeep rolling slowly, and made his way down the driveway and onto the winding mountain road.

Jeffrey stood, watching him leave, knowing he was all alone now. All alone with a woman who wouldn't hesitate to kill him if she could.

He shivered.

He turned around, and saw Rebecca in her dark gown, still wearing the black cloak, standing in the doorway of the old house. There was a smile on her face.

"Come in, Jeffrey. It's warm inside. You must be cold without your jacket, with the mist coming back, the fog returning. There's a fire inside. Come in and get warm. Come and talk to me."

A gust of cold wind from the ocean almost knocked him off his feet, causing him to stumble toward the house. And at the same time the wind howled and turned to icy fingers along his spine.

As if he was under some spell, he took willing steps toward her, toward the open door, toward the inviting voice.

Chapter 22

Rebecca had disappeared by the time Jeffrey got to the door of the house. He found her sitting cross-legged in front of the blazing fire in the living room.

The living room had been transformed with dozens of flickering candles around the wall. The effect softened the rotting draperies and peeling wallpaper. The dim light and crackling fire made for a strange, seductive setting.

Rebecca's hair billowed in a soft cloud around her face, framing cheeks rosy from the intense heat of the flames. She gave off an incandescent glow, almost as if she was a part of the fire, as if the flames came from inside. Her smile as she turned to him was warm, inviting. She held out her hand to him, indicating that he sit beside her on the floor.

Jeffrey found that despite what she had done, he was still fascinated by this woman. She had an unearthly beauty he'd never seen before. And something about her drew him to her and held him there against his will.

Remembering Tony, his anger returned. "Rebecca, don't you realize that Tony almost drowned? And that Miranda is on her way to the hospital right now with a broken leg? You are responsible for both accidents, and now you want me to forget that. You act as if nothing was your fault."

"I would have to say we share the blame, Jeffrey." Rebecca stared at the fire for a few moments, then turned to Jeffrey again and smiled.

"Yes, because I trusted you," Jeffrey said. "I let Tony think you were my friend. I didn't warn him that you were evil, Rebecca Webster."

"Evil? You accuse *me* of being evil, Jeffrey Thomas? You have no idea what evil can be, what evil can do when it grows and festers inside people, when it twists minds and spreads like a disease with no cure."

What was he doing, standing here discussing evil with Rebecca? "You killed Barbara, didn't you, Rebecca? You were on that boat, even though you denied it when you were questioned. You killed her just like you tried to kill Miranda tonight."

Rebecca turned, studied him, her face unreadable. "Only because I was killed first, Jeffrey. I have only come back to seek revenge at last."

"Come back? From where? I have no idea what you're talking about. I want you to come back into town with me. Give yourself up. You can get help, Rebecca. You need help."

He wanted her to stay calm, since he wasn't sure what she would do if she flew into another rage.

"Please don't be afraid of me, Jeffrey. Come and sit by the fire. It's a lovely fire." She patted the floor beside her.

It might be a mistake, but he moved closer and sat down. Not beside her, but on the floor in front of the blazing fire. He watched her every move, hating to admit that at the same time as he was fascinated and angry with her, he was also afraid of her. She sent his emotions billowing and crashing up and down like the ocean waves that, at this moment, battered the shore.

"That's better. Would you like to hear a story?" She stared ahead again, the fire her focus of attention. "I was so cold, always so cold. I think I can never be too warm again."

"Cold?" Rebecca still had the long black cloak around her shoulders and the room had heated nicely with the roaring fire. How could she be cold?

"When we had a fire we had to keep it small, conserve wood, ration it out slowly." She held out her hands and stared at the dancing flames. Jeffrey felt she was no longer there, in the living room of this house, but elsewhere. He waited.

"This is the last of our wood, Mercy. Do you think your husband will bring more today?"

"I fear he won't, Rebecca. We will be cold tonight when this is gone. I don't mind for myself, but it's hard to know that Dorcas is suffering."

"Perhaps we won't suffer much longer." I pull my shawl tight thinking if I get warm enough now it might last through the night. "Did you know that in England they burned witches, Mercy? We can be thankful they don't do that in Massachusetts."

Mercy Smith laughs, but without much humor. "We find strange things to be thankful for here, don't we, Rebecca?"

* * *

"I was thankful just to be warm for a few minutes."

"What are you talking about?" Jeffrey didn't understand. First Rebecca had gone into some kind of trance, now she talked about getting warm. Nothing made any sense to him.

Chapter 23

Rebecca glanced at the bare living room. "It helps me to remember that time, Jeffrey. Often you have made me forget. I didn't think that possible, but perhaps I should thank you for those precious few minutes."

The puzzled look on Jeffrey's face made her want to laugh. He had no clue to what she was talking about. On the other hand, his lack of memory made her angry. She had lived with the pain for three hundred years, while he enjoyed a life of naive joy.

It was time to tell him, to remind him, to share her reason for being here, and to bring an end to this.

She stood. Quickly he got to his feet, too. She moved slowly toward him. He backed away.

"Jeffrey! Please, it upsets me that you are

afraid. You don't really want me upset, do you?"

He couldn't speak. He shook his head and stared at her. She looked up at him and her arms circled his neck, pulling him down to kiss her. How could he kiss her? How could he not? He let himself be taken in by her spell, to sink deeper and deeper into the warm embrace.

By the time he was able to break away, to gain his senses, it was too late. He never knew how it happened . . . how she did it. There were a few moments of blackness and when he was totally aware again, his hands were tied.

"What? — "

"I have a story to tell you, Jeffrey. My hands were tied once, too."

She pushed him down to sit again, beside the fire, but it did little to warm him.

"What do you know about your ancestors, Jeffrey?" she asked, staring at him.

"What?" *What* was she talking about?

"Your family has always lived in Winthrop, haven't they, Jeffrey?"

"I — I guess so. Or Salem."

"Today not many people stay in one place. But you owned land here, lots of land, the land you took from them."

"From whom? Who took land?" He tried

154

to reason with her. "What are you talking about?"

"Patience, Jeffrey, patience. Do you know what they did for a living? Your people, your ancestors?"

"I — I think they were involved with the law, lawyers, judges. What difference does that make? What are you getting at?"

"Exactly. You come by your interest in the law naturally, Jeffrey. You were going to follow in their footsteps. I wonder if you would have made a better judge. Would you have been less rigid, more willing to hear both sides?"

"None of this talk makes sense, Rebecca."

"Caleb Thomas, Jeffrey. Does the name mean anything to you? Judge Caleb Thomas. A man of the law. A man who was supposed to be unbiased, to hear all sides and be fair in his judgment. Nothing was fair, Jeffrey. Nothing!"

Rebecca pointed her finger at him, the cape billowing around her. "I was not guilty. An innocent woman was killed, many innocent women were killed."

Her anger sent her spinning back, remembering the curse she had placed on Caleb Thomas, the reason for her return to Winthrop now. The reason she must punish Jeffrey Thomas.

"You fools! You will all die a little inside when I die. You will all lose a piece of your soul by being here, accusing me falsely, enjoying my death. I curse you all!"

A murmur of disbelief runs rapidly through the crowd. How dare she speak thus when she should be contrite and die begging for forgiveness?

Caleb Thomas frowns, his arms crossed tightly across his chest.

"I curse you especially, Caleb Thomas," I yell. "I curse you and all your descendants. I will return and seek my revenge on your sons and their sons, and the sons of those sons. You will rue the day you ever met Rebecca Webster."

The crowd shrinks back. Even Caleb Thomas's eyes hold a smattering of fear at my words.

Jeffrey Thomas's eyes held fear when Rebecca looked at him now, and she relished that fear, enjoyed being the person to make him regret the day she returned to Winthrop.

Jeffrey could see Rebecca drifting in and out of reality. Once more she had left him for several minutes, returning with her face contorted with anger, her eyes wild with pain.

"Untie me, Rebecca." Jeffrey kept his voice soft, coaxing her back to this house, reminding her of what she had done. "I won't hurt you. I promise. I'll help you. I'll take you into town where we can get some help for you. No one will hurt you."

"That's right. No one will ever hurt me again. But I can see that you still don't understand. You are so dense, Jeffrey Thomas, so stupid." She laughed. "Don't you see that I'm the only one who can carry out that curse."

"What curse, Rebecca? I don't know what curse you're talking about. And what do my ancestors have to do with you? What does it matter who I am?"

"Aha, a small light in your brain. A small window opens to the past. Thomas, Jeffrey. Caleb Thomas. Jeffrey Thomas."

"Yes, I think Caleb Thomas was a distant ancestor of mine."

"Have you never bothered to read about him, about what he did?" She clenched her fists.

"No. What does it matter?"

She let out a long sigh of frustration. "Caleb Thomas was one of the judges in the witch trials at Salem, Jeffrey. He sent many of my friends to the gallows. He sent Dorcas Smith, age four, to be hanged, but not until she had watched her mother swing from the tree on Gallows Hill. He sent Patience Clark to die because she had hair the color of the flames you see before you. Red hair! He sent my best friend, Sarah Hooker, to die because her mother was deemed a witch, spreading small-pox to the people of Salem."

"I — I didn't know."

"Did you ever bother to find out? Have you never *heard* of the witch trials of Salem?" she asked.

"Yes, I've heard of them. Everyone has heard of them."

"But people no longer care. You don't care what happened. You don't even care what happened to me."

Jeffrey kept shaking his head. "What happened to you, Rebecca?" I must keep her talking, he thought, until I figure out what this is about.

"I was next, Jeffrey. Caleb Thomas sentenced me to hang because I was Sarah's friend. Nothing I could say would save me. I was doomed. Just as you are doomed!"

I smile as the rope tightens. I welcome the fire at my throat until the thick knot chokes off my laughter.

* * *

Finally he understood what she was talking about. She thought she was from the past, living it over again. Her delusion had sent her spinning back three hundred years, thinking she was a victim of the Salem witch trials. Carefully he said, "You were hanged as a witch, Rebecca?"

"Yes, Jeffrey."

"Caleb Thomas, one of my ancestors, was the judge at your trial?" Somehow she thought she had to punish him because of what this man had done three hundred years ago. He had no idea how she had come around to thinking that she was one of the women accused of witchcraft. But clearly she believed this strongly.

"I promised him I would get revenge for his part in that evil time, Jeffrey. I have come back here to do that. In many ways I'm truly sorry you are involved. I have come to like you, Jeffrey." She smiled. "In fact, I almost fell in love with you. But I can't. You see that now."

He nodded. Yes, he could see why she had pulled away from him. Thinking what she did, she could never let herself care for him. But what had happened to her to make her believe this strange story?

"I understand how you feel, Rebecca," Jeffrey said, his voice soft and soothing again. He must get her to calm down. "I understand how you would be angry. But you don't have to do whatever it is you're planning to do."

"But I do, Jeffrey." Rebecca spun around, her skirts and cloak billowing out around her. "Not only do I have to do this, but I *want* to do it. *I want my revenge.*"

She picked up a slender branch from the wood Paul and Tony had gathered and piled in a corner near the fireplace.

Holding the stick in the fire, she waited until it flamed like a huge match. She ran to the window where a ragged old drapery hung in tatters. In addition to rotting, the drapes were as dry as cornstalks in October.

Within seconds greedy flames shot up to the ceiling, spread out to the old, peeling wall paper. It would be only a few minutes until the entire room burst into flames.

Chapter 24

"Rebecca, no!" Jeffrey tried to get to his feet. He had almost succeeded when Rebecca pushed him back down. He fell hard, stunned. Shaking his head, he tried to clear his mind, to gain his senses enough to try again.

In the light from the candles on the mantel and around the fireplace and the flames from the window and the east wall, he could see her face. Her eyes reflected the fire until they were almost red. She seemed energized by the flames and heat, the roar and crackle as the fire spread.

She spun around and around. "Jeffrey, oh, Jeffrey, at last, at last."

He started to cough as smoke filled the room. "Rebecca! Please! Let's get out of here."

Jeffrey kept looking for a way to get his hands free or to get to his feet again. He could run with his hands tied. But Rebecca spun and whirled between him and the door, her black cloak and dress billowing around her, blocking the door.

She had no intention of letting him go. Finally he realized that. She planned to kill him, to get revenge for this fantasy she had dreamed up. He was to blame for her anguish, whether real or imagined. He took a chance and rolled toward the window, even though that was the last way out. Rebecca screamed and dashed toward him.

Like a crazy, out-of-control top, he spun around and rolled away when he could no longer stand the intense heat, and when he risked catching on fire himself.

Watching him, Rebecca forgot to look out for herself. Her skirt swung through the flames, igniting with a whoosh.

Closing off all thought of her as a woman, or a friend that he could help, Jeffrey flipped to his feet, tilted forward, then back, caught his balance and pounded toward the door of the living room.

Once in the hall, he stuck out his foot, swung the door closed, heard the latch click. Then he leaned on the door with all his weight. Rebecca still might push it open. She seemed possessed of incredible strength.

"Jeffrey, help!" She pounded on the door. He could feel the thudding of her fists. He gritted his teeth and resisted giving in to her cries.

He bit his lip, closed his eyes, and bent over to bear the pain that shot through his whole body at the thought of what he was doing to her. But he didn't stop holding the door closed.

Finally, when he heard nothing else but the roar of the fire, eating its way through the old walls, he dashed for the front door.

To his amazement, a key remained in the front lock. He turned his back, yanked the key into both hands, then stepped outside. With his foot, he reached for the door to close it.

Only when he was several feet away from the house did he spin around and look back.

Through the panes of the French door, he saw the face of Rebecca Webster. He was amazed that she was still on her feet, still alive. And to his surprise, her face didn't register pain but terrible anger and hatred.

As much as he wanted to look away, he continued to stare at the face at the door. He watched until she seemed to fade away into the smoke and fire.

At that moment, when he knew she was gone, the tears slid down his face. Tears for Rebecca! Tears for Barbara. Obsessed by Rebecca, he had not mourned Barbara properly. Perhaps now he could.

The tears had a cleansing effect. It was as if he had truly been under some spell which only now, with Rebecca's death, was broken.

"Jeffrey!" A voice reached him over the roar of the fire. "Are you all right? What happened?"

Paul dashed up beside Jeffrey and grabbed his arm. "How — Where is — "

"She's in there. She must surely be dead by now. I — I couldn't — " No, that was a lie. He hadn't tried to save Rebecca. He was too busy saving himself. "She tried to kill me, Paul. She set the place on fire and planned to leave me in there. I got away from her. She was caught in her own trap."

"You're tied up." Paul had just noticed. "How did you get out of there with your hands tied?" Paul started unfastening the knots around Jeffrey's wrists. He held up the cord that had been around Jeffrey's wrists. *It was a black velvet ribbon!*

Jeffrey stared at it in disbelief. He shook his hands to start the circulation through them. "What are you doing here? I thought you were at the hospital with Miranda."

"I was. I took her there, but she wouldn't let me stay. As soon as someone was taking care of her, she sent me back. She said you'd need my help." Paul stared at the house, now totally encased in flames. Old and decayed, the entire structure, even with recent rains, had been so dry it succumbed easily to the fire.

"Let's get out of here, Paul. We'll send the fire department back to put this out and make sure it doesn't spread into the woods." Jeffrey started for the car.

"Jeffrey" — Paul put his hand on Jeffrey's arm, stopping him — "Miranda made me promise one more thing before I returned to the hospital. She said, if I found you, if I wasn't too late, that she wanted you to see something. A grave in the old pioneer cemetery."

Jeffrey started walking the short distance away from the house to where a number of old gravestones still stood. Paul followed.

"Miranda said this might explain Rebecca's anger. Did Miranda tell you that twice she found Rebecca wandering in the cemetery, looking at the graves? And that once she stood before one of them, crying?"

"No, she never told me that." Jeffrey looked around. The night was the clearest he'd seen all summer. Even this near the ocean, there wasn't a wisp of fog in the air. It was as if the fire and smoke had burned off the mist. A full moon rose high, laying down a path of silver for them to follow.

Even stranger was how the moon lit up the graveyard. The crumbling stones cast long shadows, but one grave in particular glowed in a cold, silver spotlight.

"Look, Jeffrey," Paul whispered.

The gravestone they stared at was easy to read, even now, three hundred years after the words had been carved in the stone.

> OUR DAUGHTER
> REBECCA WEBSTER
> 1675–1692
> FALSELY ACCUSED
> DIED ON THE GALLOWS
> MAY SHE REST IN PEACE

Again Paul whispered, just loud enough for Jeffrey to hear. "Miranda thinks this may have been a distant ancestor of Rebecca's. That's why Rebecca came to Winthrop."

Jeffrey bit his bottom lip and felt the tears slide down his cheeks. An ancestor? Maybe not. But what he was thinking? What Rebecca had said wasn't possible! Was it? "I don't know." He brushed his face with his sleeve.

"Jeffrey? Come on, let's go."

"I'm coming." Jeffrey let Paul start back,

but he lingered for a moment more, staring at the words, remembering Rebecca's story.

"I don't know. But Rebecca, if that *was* you, I'm sorry, and I did love you."

Jeffrey turned, headed back to the glow in the clearing. With the car door open, he stood, staring. The old house had tumbled in on itself, the fire seemed contained. Nothing of the structure remained. No one could have escaped.

"Rebecca," he whispered. "Rest in peace."

Salem, 1692
Seventeen-year-old Rebecca is hanged as a witch.

Now
Rebecca's back—and ready for revenge.

DARK MOON

**A two-part saga
by Elizabeth Moore**

Jeffrey loves Rebecca, but he suspects that
something isn't quite right. The closer he gets to
her, the more she runs away. Will Rebecca be able
to enjoy her love—or is the pain of her fatal past
driving her to a new doom?

**Book #1: KISS OF DEATH
Book #2: DREAMS OF REVENGE**

DM11/94

High on a hill,
trapped in the shadows,
something inside a dark house
is waiting...and watching.

THE HOUSE ON CHERRY STREET

**A three-book series
by Rodman Philbrick and Lynn Harnett**

Terror has a new home—and the children
are the only ones who sense it—from the
blasts of icy air in the driveway, to the windows
that shut like guillotines. Can Jason and Sally
stop the evil that lives in the dark?

**Book #1: THE HAUNTING
Book #2: THE HORROR
Book #3: THE FINAL NIGHTMARE**

HCS1194